Claiming Mia
C.A.P.E. INVESTIGATIONS
BOOK 1
DEANNA L. ROWLEY

I'd like to thank, my editor, Ann Attwood, for the wonderful job she does on my books.

Table of Contents

CHAPTER ONE
Eagan

"I'll get it!" Eagan Davenport called out when the doorbell peeled through the house. He whipped open the door and grinned at the man standing there. Reaching into his pocket, he pulled out a twenty-dollar bill and handed it over. "Thanks, man. I was worried that you wouldn't make it."

"Sorry about that. I had a flat tire and had to change it." The man held out his hands as he passed the delivery over, and Eagan winced at his bloody knuckles.

"Ouch." Eagan pointed to the man's hand. "Hopefully, you don't have many more deliveries."

"Only three more after you. Better get going," the man said as he turned and hurried down the steps.

With his arms full, Eagan backed into the house. As he turned, he grinned when he saw two hands come to his rescue.

"What in the world?" His mother, Meg Davenport, asked from across the room. "What do you need with all those flowers, Eagan?"

Eagan grinned at his mother as he and his father placed them on the kitchen counter. He turned to her and laughed. "This dozen of red roses are for you." He chuckled when he saw his mother's shocked expression. Continuing, he said, "This is the wrist corsage for Sue Ellen for tonight. And this dozen of multi-colored roses are for Mrs. Tavers."

"Wow," David, Eagan's father, said. "I can understand the ones for Sue Ellen, but why your mother and Mrs. Tavers?"

Eagan shrugged. "Why not?" He picked up the dozen red roses, carried them across the room, and placed them in his mother's arms. "Thank you for being the mother you are. I love you." He kissed her cheek and grinned when his father swore, pulled his handkerchief from his pocket, and went to his wife, glaring at his son.

"Really? You know your mother is a powerful woman. Her only two weaknesses are you and red roses. Now, I have to see if I can outdo this." His tone conveyed disgust, but his facial expression showed glee, and he high-fived his son as he walked by to get to his wife. With Meg wrapped in his arms, he looked at his son. "What exactly are your plans for tonight?"

"Well, I'm sure you know it's the Senior Prom?" Eagan asked, and laughed when both his parents rolled their eyes at him. "I'm picking Sue Ellen up at five thirty. We have dinner reservations for six. Four other couples are joining us. After dinner, we'll go back to school for the dance. Again, last I heard, the after-party is at Davis's place."

"Who?" Meg asked, as she lifted her nose from the roses with a frown.

"Davis Hollingsworth. He moved here this past summer. His father's in the Marines, and Davis said he wanted to finish his schooling in the States. Once we graduate, he will visit his parents and siblings in Japan, then join the Marines in the fall. He's living with his grandparents until school's out."

"Won't it be too much to have a bunch of rowdy teenagers at their place?" David frowned at his son.

"I don't think so. His grandparents are the Hadleys, six blocks over." Eagan pointed in the general direction of where the after-party would be.

"Midge and Gerald have their grandson living with them?" Meg frowned at her husband.

"I guess so," David answered with a frown. He looked at his wife and sighed. "I admit we haven't been around much in the last few weeks, especially with our workload. I must get over there sometime soon and see how they're doing." He turned to his son and nodded. "You know I don't have to tell you how to conduct yourself tonight? I trust you, and I trust that your manners will be impeccable."

"That's a given. I'll be on my utmost behavior. Before you ask, there will be no alcohol present. That was the only thing Davis stressed when he invited people over. We know the police will be out and about. This close to graduation, no one wants to lose a friend to a stupid tragic accident. None of us at the Prom or party are over eighteen, except for Mr. and Mrs. Hadley. I know they won't be serving any alcohol." Eagan looked at his watch, then grinned. "I'm going to excuse myself to get ready for my date." He left his parents standing there looked at each other.

"It's only three in the afternoon. Since when does it take our son over two hours to get ready for anything?" Meg laughed at her husband. She took her roses to the kitchen and quickly snipped the ends before putting them in a vase. She dug around in the back of the cupboards and found another vase.

Pruning the roses for Sue Ellen's mother the same way she had hers, she arranged them for Eagan to take later.

David came up from behind her and put his arms around her, giving her a tight squeeze. "Can I ask you something?"

"Sure, what's up?"

"Do you think Eagan will ever get the hint that Roc is in love with him? I thought for sure he would have asked her to the Senior Prom, instead of Sue Ellen."

"Why?" Meg frowned as she turned in her husband's arms. "E and Sue Ellen have been dating for two years. Why would he break it off with her to go out with someone who he only considers a sister?"

David jerked in shock. "Really? But you can see that she loves him."

"She may love him, but he doesn't love her." Meg sighed. "I asked him about it after he asked Sue Ellen to go steady with him. He flat out said that he loves Roc, but he isn't in love with her. He also stressed the love he felt for her was as a sibling. Not as a man loves a woman, he wants to marry. But then again, he also admitted that he cared deeply for Sue Ellen, but he didn't see a future for the two of them after high school." Meg studied her husband and frowned at his expression.

"What?"

"Nothing."

"David." Meg drew the word out. When he sighed, she knew he would finally talk to her.

"It's just that Bradley said something that Roc is letting Eagan sow his oats before he realizes that she is the one for him. He even mentioned that she's going to the same college as him."

"No, they accepted her at Berkley. Shelby, her mother, told everyone at the club, her daughter would go to Berkley after high school. She wants to become a lawyer. According to Shelby, it's Berkley for pre-law, then on to Harvard for the law degree."

"Bradley told me she was going to UB this fall."

"I wonder if E knows."

"No clue."

DRAWING IN A DEEP BREATH before letting it out slowly, Eagan raised his hand and knocked on Sue Ellen Tavers's front door. Mr. Tavers opened the door and stepped back to invite the younger man in.

"Eagan, welcome," Mr. Tavers said as he stepped back. He frowned at the enormous bouquet of roses the younger man held. His first thought was, why would he give something like that to his daughter. "Sue Ellen will be down in a minute."

"Thank you, Mr. Tavers. Is Mrs. Tavers home?"

"Yes, she's upstairs with Sue Ellen."

"Thank you." Eagan suddenly felt nervous. "I hope I'm not stepping on any toes here, but I'd like to give these to Mrs. Tavers." He held out the vase of flowers his mother had fixed for him. Just then, Mrs. Tavers walked in.

"What beautiful flowers."

"They're for you," Mr. Tavers said and handed them to his wife. Before he could say anything, she hurried forward and put her arms around him, giving him a kiss. Eagan didn't say a word to correct her assumption that her husband bought them for her. He looked up the stairs and saw Sue Ellen standing there in her Prom dress. Leaving the older couple's side, he stepped forward and held out his hand toward his girlfriend. Sue Ellen was beautiful. With dark-blonde hair done up and only a few curls framing her face, she took his breath away.

"Beautiful," Eagan whispered. Her dress was pale blue with sparkles on the bodice. And it was strapless. He swallowed his tongue when he saw her cleavage. He had never seen her look more beautiful. Once she reached the bottom of the stairs, he held out the corsage and put it on her wrist. It surprised Eagan when it was Mr. Tavers that pulled out a camera and began snapping pictures.

"Dad," Sue Ellen laughed. "You can stop now. We have dinner reservations."

"Oh, okay." The older man grinned, then snapped more pictures. Sue Ellen's brother joined them to take photos of the two couples. When they finally left, both Eagan and Sue Ellen were laughing.

"You'd think he'd never seen one of his kids to go to the prom before," Sue Ellen said as they walked to Eagan's car. He helped her in and looked at her.

"But you're the first girl. I'm sure your two older brothers went to their dates' homes and had pictures taken there."

"There is that," Sue Ellen admitted, and sighed in happiness as she put her seatbelt on. Once Eagan started driving, she bit her lower lip, and asked, "So, who's all joining us tonight?"

"Roc, Davis, Jeremy, and Ben, along with their dates."

Sue Ellen said nothing for some time. She waited until they parked at the restaurant. After Eagan shut off the car, she laid her hand on his forearm to prevent him from getting out.

"I will not fight with you. I know how much Roc means to you, but please, for me, will you keep your eyes open around her? Watch her. I know you classify her as your best friend, and you have no romantic feelings toward her. But that's not how she feels about you. I've heard a rumor that she's following you to UB in the fall for college."

"No, she's going to Berkley." Eagan frowned at his date. He didn't want to argue either. He never understood why his friends always warned him about his best friend. Sure, she was a female, but Rochelle Mason was only that. There had been no romantic feelings for her in all the time they'd lived across the street from each other, which happened to be since the day they were both brought home from the hospital. It turned out Eagan was precisely twelve hours older than Rochelle. Living in the same neighborhood, they grew up together, went to school together, and had the same friends. It was just that Eagan had no romantic feelings for her, other than a deep friendship.

Rubbing his forehead, he studied his girlfriend intently. When she didn't back down from his stare, he looked out the windshield, then back to look at her. "What aren't you telling me?"

"Are you sure you want to know?"

Eagan studied his girlfriend of two years and sighed. Not once in all the time they dated had she ever lied to him. "I trust you."

"Good." Sue Ellen didn't hesitate. She turned in her seat to face Eagan. Taking her hand in his, she gripped it hard. "I love you, Eagan." She held up her hand when he tried to say something. "But not in the way our parents love each other. As much as I love you, I don't want to marry you. It's not that kind of love. Do you understand?"

"Yes, I feel the same way, Sue Ellen. I love you, but I'm not *in* love with you."

"Exactly. We both have plans after graduation. I don't want to mess those up. I see myself as a lawyer someday. And you're going to be a cop."

"I'm not quite sure about that yet." Eagan grinned at her.

"But you are going for the Criminal Justice degree, right?"

"Correct, but I don't know if I want to be a cop or to join the FBI."

"See, and we both know that if we married, then those plans would be out the window." She looked at him, grinned, and giggled. "That's why I have you double up on the condoms."

Eagan laughed. "And that's why you have that device. No way are we getting pregnant. Not that I wouldn't be there for you, but still."

"I understand. But from what I've observed, seen with my own eyes, and told directly, Roc is in love with you."

"I don't understand how. I have no romantic feelings for her."

"The day I went shopping for this dress." Sue Ellen pointed to the dress she wore. "I ran into Roc. She flat-out told me she was allowing you to sow your wild oats in high school, because that was what every dutiful wife did. But once you are at college together, all bets are off, and you are finally going to be hers." Sue Ellen held up her hands to ward off Eagan's anger. "Like I just said to you. I will always tell you the truth. She's deeply in love with you. I have a feeling that if something happens, and you meet your Mrs. Right, she's going to fuck it up. So, this is just a brief word of advice. Don't let her walk all over your Mrs. Right. Stick up for her. If you really love whoever your future is to be with, then let her know. Aaand..." She drew the word out until she knew she had his full attention. "If anything happens, know that I will be there for you. Even if you only want to rant and rave at what a bitch Roc is."

Eagan drew in a deep breath and let it out slowly. "Not that I don't believe you, but I can't see anything like that happening. She does not turn me on sexually nor romantically. Not like you do." He grinned, then leaned in and kissed her. They didn't break apart until several people began pounding on their car. They looked up and saw the rest of their dinner party had arrived. Eagan quickly jumped out of the car, ran around, and helped Sue Ellen out. He glanced around the group and noticed that Roc only looked at him. Her expression made him wonder if maybe Sue Ellen was right. But he lost that thought as they all greeted one another and made their way into the restaurant.

CHAPTER TWO
ROCHELLE

Rochelle Mason waved her hand at the two women in her bedroom like they were a nuisance to her. The two women were the makeup artist and hairstylist her mother had hired to help get her ready for her Senior Prom. If she hadn't been such a courteous person, her date would have been the love of her life, Eagan Cunningham. Not only had Rochelle been in love with him for as long as she could remember, but if she kept her cool, it would be only a few weeks before they would be together. She only allowed him to date Sue Ellen Tavers while in high school, because she knew they liked each other, but not so much that they would make plans to marry after graduation. If that had been the case, Roc would have stepped in months ago.

No, Rochelle held the position of Eagan's future wife. Eagan just didn't know it yet. Months ago, Rochelle, "Roc" Mason had received an acceptance letter from Berkley in California. The day she'd stood next to her mailbox to open her acceptance letter was the day she walked across the street and rifled through the Cunningham mailbox. Since no one said a word, she'd hurried back to her own home, steamed the letter open, and read it. She stood next to her mailbox when Eagan had returned from school. Together, they met in the middle of the street and compared acceptance letters.

Roc and Eagan had been best friends all their lives. If it wasn't for her mother's laziness, they would have the same birthday. Eagan had been born at eleven thirty-five at night. Exactly twelve hours later, at eleven thirty-five the next morning, Roc had been born. Rochelle resented her mother for her lack of consideration for not giving birth to her earlier.

The day she and Eagan compared college acceptance letters, he'd given her a hug and said that he would miss her. Since she was his best friend. Later that night, instead of doing her homework, she'd filled out the application to the University of Buffalo and overnighted it the next day. She told no one that they had accepted her. She was saving that surprise for when she arrived on campus and saw Eagan for the first time. She couldn't wait to get him all to herself.

Rochelle sighed as she stood and leaned into the mirror, giving herself a critical once over. She liked what she saw. Even if she said so herself, she was a beautiful woman with blonde hair and blue eyes. Her tits weren't as big as she'd like, but she had an appointment for three days after her high school graduation. That was when her breast enlargement surgery would take place. The summer would suck with her healing, but she'd be able to surprise Eagan when she arrived at college. She knew he'd take one look at her larger breasts and fall over her. She'd be one size bigger than Sue Ellen now. Her mother would get some work down along with her, so they rented a place in LA for the summer. It was all lined up, along with the people to wait on them. It was Rochelle's goal to be a perfect size two when she arrived at college. She was a four now, but along with her boob job, she had convinced her mother to let her get a tummy tuck also. The doctor tried to talk her out of having both major surgeries simultaneously, but Rochelle always got what she wanted. Always. This turned out to be no different.

There was a knock on her door, and she called for the person to enter. Gretchen, the maid, entered with a black garment bag. She entered, unzipped it, then presented the white, strapless dress.

"Stunning," the makeup artist said. When she reached out to touch it, Rochelle slapped her hand so hard, it left a red mark.

"Don't fucking touch it, bitch. That's mine. Nobody touches what's mine." Rochelle snarled at the other woman. Both the makeup artist and hairdresser finished packing their things, then left the room. Neither of them saw the expression of pity on Gretchen's face.

"Hard to find good help these days," Rochelle growled, then dropped her robe. Beneath she wore only a white thong, garter, and sheer stockings. She didn't wear a bra because she was only an A-cup, so didn't really need one. In a few weeks she would sport firm D-cups. She couldn't wait. Gretchen never said a word as she helped Rochelle into her dress. She had worked for the Masons for almost twenty years and knew what a bitch the younger girl could be. Her father knew too, because when he asked Gretchen to do extra "Roc duty," as he called it, she received a bonus in her pay. This night would guarantee her another massive bonus.

Once Rochelle dressed entirely, Gretchen quickly left to head downstairs. She nodded to the Masons and took the envelope Bradley handed her. "Thank you, Mr. Mason."

"How bad was it?" he asked.

"An eight. Her only complaint was that her chest didn't look right in the dress."

"Thank you, Gretchen. We'll see you on Monday."

"See you on Monday, Mr. Mason. Mrs. Mason." She nodded, turned on her heel, grabbed her coat and purse and left as quickly as she could. As she drove down the road, she saw an unfamiliar car and wondered if that was Rochelle's date. God forgive her, but she wished the man would develop the stomach bug and toss his cookies all down the front of that virginal white dress that Rochelle Mason had no right wearing. There was no way that young woman was a virgin. And it wasn't speculation on her part. Not only had she seen Rochelle with different boys, but she'd had to clean the used condoms out of the wastebaskets in both the bedroom and bathroom. Giving herself a tiny shudder, she only had to last a few more weeks, then Mrs. Mason and Rochelle would be gone for the summer. The day after they left would be the day Gretchen turned in her notice. She couldn't wait.

Roc stood in front of her three-way mirror admiring herself. As she turned this way and that, she pictured her new body. Flatter stomach and bigger boobs. Sighing, she gave a start when the doorbell peeled. Waiting for ten minutes, she slowly made her way down to her date. She and Robert have been dating for the last four months. If Eagan had been available, she never would have given the time of day to the other boy. After realizing how good he was in bed, she kept him around for that purpose. That and he was her date for tonight. Rochelle also liked that he was honest with her and didn't put up with any of her shit. Again, if it hadn't been for Eagan, she believed she could learn to love Robert.

Rochelle suffered through the pictures her mother insisted on taking. After about ten minutes, she said they needed to be going, because of their dinner reservations. On the way to the car, she kept looking across the street, looking for any sign of Eagan.

"He's not there," Robert spoke from behind her, then helped her into the BMW. Once they were behind the wheel, he looked at Roc before he started the car.

"I passed E on my way here. He's probably already at Sue Ellen's. I'm only going to say this once, Rochelle. You are my date tonight. I know you're in love with Eagan Davenport. Too damn bad. But he's not in love with you, and he's with his girlfriend. This is the only warning you get. If I see you mooning over him, I'll bring you directly home. Do you understand me?"

"You're such a fucking bastard."

"I am. Now, did you understand what I said?"

"Why couldn't Eagan and I meet you guys at the restaurant. You live near that cow, you could have brought her, I could have ridden with Eagan."

Robert only stared at her, not saying a word. After four complete minutes of silence, Rochelle sighed dramatically. "I know, I know," she said sarcastically. "He's dating her."

"Exactly. You will not refer to Sue Ellen as a cow again in my presence. If you do, I'll leave you stranded wherever we are. Be it at the restaurant, the school, or even at the Hadleys.

You are my date. I expect you not only to respect me, but also everyone else. Is that understood?" Robert again remained quiet for several more minutes. "Fine, you won't answer. Get your ass out of my car now. I'll go stag."

"I understand," Rochelle quickly changed her tune when she realized how serious Robert was. If it was anyone else, she would have pushed her luck. Robert always followed through on his threats. Except they weren't threats, they were promises. And the make-up sex was absolutely out of this world. She loved his control when they were together like that.

"I said I understand," she growled at him, and Robert nodded once, started the car, and drove to the restaurant. After exiting the car, they waited for the others to join them. Robert put his arm around her shoulder and growled in her ear. "Not a word." Then he and the other guys pounded on the steamy windows of Eagan's car. They all laughed when the couple broke apart.

LATER THAT NIGHT, ROCHELLE sat at the table the ten of them had commandeered when they entered the gymnasium at the high school, and stared at the couple in the middle of the dance floor. She was seething. Not only had she not been able to be Eagan's date, but she'd lost out on being the Prom Queen as well. "Fucking cow," Rochelle said, and didn't realize Robert was standing behind her with two glasses of punch. He set them down, grabbed his suit jacket, and stared at her.

"Good luck finding a ride to the party." He turned on his heel and strode away.

"What?" Rochelle asked in shock. She jumped to her feet, not realizing that when Robert set the glasses down one of them had spilled. She stumbled and the other glass tipped over, and the front of her white silk dress became drenched in red fruit punch. She ignored it as she tore out after Robert.

"Where are you going?"

"I told you, if you called Sue Ellen a cow again tonight, I was leaving you. Don't deny it. I heard you. I'm done Roc. Your obsession with a man that will never love you is borderline crazy."

"I'm sorry."

"No. you're not. You're only sorry because you got caught. All night you've been hanging on Eagan's every word. No one can talk to you because your nose is so far up his ass you don't pay any attention to them. Thank fucking god no one elected you Prom Queen."

"Why do you say that?"

"Because you would have lorded it over Sue Ellen." Robert sighed as he finally turned to look at her. They stood in the parking lot, and he didn't know if it surprised him or not that she carried her shawl and a small purse. "I voted for Eagan, and yes, I voted for Sue Ellen."

"But I'm dating you. Why would you do that to me?"

"Because you're dating me. Do you think I want to see you in the arms of another man? A man you love, but who doesn't love you back. Grow the fuck up, Rochelle. It's never going to happen. Not in a million years."

"You're wrong. I'm only allowing Eagan to sow his wild oats before we go to college. He'll see, once we're away from everyone here, he'll come around."

"Oh my god, you are such a stupid fool." Robert shook his head. "Now, get in the car, and I'll take you home."

"Why would I want you to do that?" Roc practically screamed at him.

"Do you want to go back inside, looking like that?" He pointed to her dress, and as she looked down, she did scream when she saw the red stain on the front of her dress.

"What the fucking hell!" Rochelle screamed. "Oh my god, can tonight get any worse?" she asked the rhetorical question. Turning her wrath toward Robert, he held up his hands.

"I warned you before we even left your house. You knew what would happen if you allowed your true colors to show. I'm sick and tired of trying to play second fiddle to a man who will never see you as you see him. Do you know why I keep saying that? Because I flat-out asked Eagan before I asked you out if he had any problems with us dating. Do you want to know his answer?"

"What?" Rochelle held her breath, waiting to hear what Robert had to say.

"He told me to go for it. When I asked if he had any designs on you, he laughed. He laughed so hard he had tears rolling down his face. His exact words to me were, *"Why the hell would I care if you date my sister?"* Did you hear what I said, Rochelle? He sees you as a sister. Not as a woman he could have any type of romantic relationship with. If you can't get past that, then I feel sorry for you. Last chance, am I taking you home or not?"

Rochelle exhaled and looked down at her dress. "Might as well. My night's ruined, anyway." She stormed her way to the side of the vehicle and stared in shock when Robert didn't even bother opening the door for her. He got into the driver's side, then leaned over and opened the door. She got in and fumed the twenty minutes to her home. Before she could get out, he left the doors locked and said nothing until she looked at him.

"I'm done, Rochelle. I'm breaking up with you. Your obsession with Eagan is sick. You need professional help. Block my number from your phone. Never call me again unless you've gotten over this sickness of yours. Have a nice life." He unlocked the doors and watched as she exited the car. She barely slammed the door shut before he was backing out of the driveway. Since the dance had almost been over, he drove the six blocks over to the Hadleys, and wasn't surprised that many people had already arrived. It shocked him when, hours later, not one person asked where Rochelle was. He smirked when he realized that their classmates didn't even care enough to ask after her.

Rochelle stormed out of Robert's car, pissed off with the world. Not only at Robert for calling her out on calling Sue Ellen a cow, but also for breaking up with her. How dare he, what right did he have to judge her? Storming inside, she slammed the back door and ignored her parents as she stormed up the stairs. As she jerked her dress off, it ripped. Too pissed to realize what she was doing, she grabbed the ripped parts and finished tearing it with her hand. By the time she finished, the dress was in tatters, with no hope of ever repairing it. There wasn't even a piece of material big enough to use as a dust rag. She finished undressing and stormed into her bathroom. In less than twenty minutes, she'd washed the nightmare of her night off.

Back out in her room, Rochelle dressed in one of Eagan's tee shirts she'd taken off their clothesline years ago. With him being so much bigger than she, she used it as a nightshirt. Not that she wore it every night, but when she was having a bad time, she wore it. It made her think he was hugging her, trying to soothe her foul mood. Feeling the material settle around her, for the first time in hours, Rochelle could take a deep calming breath. She pulled her diary and wrote all the horrid things that happened to her that night.

How Robert had accused her of being a sick stalker, how that fat cow, Sue Ellen had stolen her date out from under her, along with her title of Prom Queen. As she wrote how she would pay them back for their sins against her, Rochelle finally calmed down enough to pull her phone and look at the photos she'd taken of Eagan that night. Going to her computer, she downloaded the images, cropped Sue Ellen out of them, and added herself.

"We are a beautiful couple, Eagan. If it's the last thing I ever do, you will finally see that we belong together. No woman will ever come between us. There will be hell to pay to any bitch stupid enough to take you away from me. You are mine, and if you're stupid enough not to realize that, no other woman will ever have you."

Rochelle spent several hours adjusting tonight's photos to her satisfaction. After she crawled into bed, she fell asleep to a picture of Eagan holding a rose toward her. Who gave a shit that she stood behind Sue Ellen to take the picture? The fat cow was in the way anyway. Eagan was hers. Soon she would learn the truth. God forbid anyone come between them once they were away at college.

CHAPTER THREE
MIA

Mia Cunningham stood in the doorway to her parents' shared office and sighed. She had been standing there for fifteen minutes, and not once had they looked up to acknowledge her. Grasping the paper firmly in her hand, she strode in, and stopped before her father's desk. When he still didn't look up, she put her forms in front of him. "Sign these."

When Guthrie Cunningham tried to push the papers aside, Mia leaned over, placed her hand on them, and said through gritted teeth. "Sign these." He finally looked up and frowned at her.

"What are you doing? You know you're not allowed in here."

"Father, I'm sixteen years old. You and mother have buried yourselves in your work for the last twelve hours. I've stood at the door, calling both your names for the last twenty minutes. I need you to sign these." She shook the papers in his face.

"What are they?"

"Don't worry about them. Sign, and I'll get out of your hair."

Guthrie tossed his pen on his desk, leaned back, and rubbed the bridge of his nose. He looked at his daughter and frowned. He barely recognized her. "As a lawyer, you know I will sign nothing until I read them."

"Fine, then read the damn papers, sign them, and hand them back." Mia had learned at an early age to stick up for herself, or her parents would never realize that she was around. That was why she had signed up for the debate club two years ago. She wanted her voice and opinions heard. It took one semester as a sophomore in high school, but she was now the debate team captain. In her school, usually, only seniors held that position.

"What am I reading?"

"College admission forms."

"No," Guthrie said. He never even picked them up to read. "You will not be going to college."

"Why not? It's not like we can't afford it. If we can't, I'm sure I can get grants or student loans."

"You're too young to think about college. You have a few years yet."

"I'll be seventeen on my next birthday. I have six weeks left of school this year. Then I'll be a junior. I have two years left of high school. There's no time like the present to get the applications filled out and sent in." When Mia saw her father's expression, she stood tall on her five foot three frame. She drew in a deep breath and began, "Are you going to deny your only child the right to further her education? Both you and mom have college degrees. You are a lawyer. Mom is an architect. Why don't you want me to go to college?"

"You're too young."

"Wrong answer, Father."

"Since when have you started calling me 'Father?' I've always been Dad to you."

"Since you started being a butthead." Mia glared at the man behind his desk, then paced. "Your argument of me being too young will not fly. I want concrete evidence of why you won't sign the papers to send my application in. Remember, before you answer, I'll be eighteen in fifty-four weeks. You have no say in my life after that." Mia paused and stared at her father. This next point she wanted to make, she had to nail it down, or she would blow the whole thing. She knew how her parents operated.

"You and mother grew up in the seventies, eighties, and nineties. You met in college, you partied, you got the best education your parents could buy. Why are you denying me the opportunity to do as you did? Get an education, find the love of my life, and have a happily ever after. I refuse to accept your answer, stating that I'm too young."

Guthrie stared at his daughter, rubbed the back of his neck, and looked at Midge, his wife. "Since when did she get so argumentative?"

"No clue, dear," Midge answered without looking up from her computer.

"Why did you two even have me?" Mia asked out loud. She had always wondered why. They were both the same age, and Mia hadn't been born until they were in their early forties. "You ignore me like you don't care. You should have given me up for adoption or had an abortion. I would have been better off than what little affection the two of you give me." She grabbed the papers from her father's desk, tore them in half, and threw them back at him. "Fine, I'll go stand on a street corner to get my education." After turning and storming away, she made sure the office door slammed shut behind her. Who cared that it sprang back open and hit the wall behind it, then actually slammed shut? She only wanted to get her point across. This kind of behavior had never come from her before.

Guthrie looked over at his wife and noticed for the first time she'd looked up from her computer. He picked up the papers his daughter had torn and tossed at him. As he pieced them back together, he frowned. Looking back at his wife, he asked, "Midge, since when has Mia been on the debate team?"

"What? I didn't know she was." Midge stood and went over and read the application over her husband's shoulder. "Wow, I didn't know she was into half of these things."

Guthrie stood, walked to the door to the office. After he opened it, he yelled, "MIA! Come here, please."

Five minutes later, Mia walked in, but said nothing. She took a seat and remained quiet.

"I'm going to get right to the point," her father said. "How do I know you're not lying about these activities you have listed here?"

Mia saw red. She lifted her head and glared at her father. "If you'd bother to realize you have a child and maybe spent time with me, you would realize those activities are real. Don't you think the teachers or principal would call and tell you if those were lies? Not only am I the president of the debate team, but I'm the president of my class. I'm also on the National Honor Society. I have a three-point-nine-eight grade average. As of right now, I'm in the lead for being valedictorian."

"You never told us any of this." Her mother frowned. The tone of her voice indicated to Mia that they didn't believe her.

"You're never home." Mia shot back. "Both of you are either at work, with a client, or in here. Not once have you ever been to any of my debates. Nor have you been to a parent-teacher conference since I was in the third grade. You do everything on the computer. So, Father," she sniped at him. "You telling me I'm too young to go to college, what do you care? You're never here, anyway. Neither are you, Mom. I'm not trying to be a bitch, but I have never asked you for anything in my life. Even when I was younger. I knew your work came first. All I'm asking is for you to sign the college application. I don't have to turn it in until September, but I really want to go to this school."

"Which one?" Guthrie asked, not bothering to look at the application. It was like he saw his daughter for the first time.

"The University of Buffalo."

"In New York State? Why would you want to go to the other side of the country? We live in Idaho. Isn't there something closer?"

"There could be, but I've always wanted to see Niagara Falls." Mia held up her hand. "I know, that's not an excuse to go to that school, but they are highly accredited. I'm about to be perfectly honest with you. I only signed up for debate to figure out how to argue. I thought if either of you lifted your head long enough to realize I was here, we could have a conversation. I am not interested in being a lawyer." Mia held up her hand when they tried to speak again. "I know how important it was for the two of you to make partner. Grandma explained it to me. Even though you inherited the firm when Grandpa died, Dad, you still had to prove yourself to the other partners. I get that. But what you forgot was that I was here growing up. I will not cry over spilled milk, but I truly wonder why you ever kept me or didn't have an abortion. You were both forty-four when I was born. I guess you could say I was a late baby. You're going to be sixty this year. What do you have to show for it? Besides this house, and the firm? Along with Mom's firm. What else? Where's the laughter? Where's the love? Where's the family time? Because it sure as hell isn't here. And don't even think about leaving me any part of your business when you die. I'll sell it to the highest bidder."

"Over our dead bodies," Midge said, with her hands on her hips.

"Yep, you'll be dead, so what do you care? I'm not a bitch, I'm really not, but someone has to look out for my future. You two may be my parents by blood, but you don't care about me, so why harass me about college? I'd have thought you'd want me out of your hair. Then you wouldn't have to worry about me. It's not like you do now." Mia sighed. She stood and shook her head. "Sorry, but I've been in a pissy mood lately, and I've taken it out on you. For that, I apologize. But I do not apologize for what I've just said. I believe every word."

"What can we do to fix this?" Guthrie asked.

Mia frowned at her father, like he'd grown a second head, along with horns and a tail. She stood there in shock, then blurted out. "Come to one of my debates. Sit and watch me. Come home from work before ten at night. Cook a meal we can all sit down and enjoy. Not fast food or take out. Something we can all cook. Fire up that thousand-dollar grill you had installed six years ago and have *not* used once. That's all I ask. Spend time as a family." Mia studied her parents and sighed. "Face it, guys, you're not getting any younger. I'll be seventeen in two weeks, and you two are almost sixty. Legally in two years, you can retire. Or you can retire now. I'll be away at college, so..." She left the sentence hanging as she rose and walked out of the home office calmer than she had earlier.

TWO WEEKS LATER, MIA was backstage at her high school auditorium pacing. It was the last debate before the finals. If they won today, then their school would go to the finals. This would be the first time in the school's history they had gone this far. Drawing in a deep breath, she let it out slowly and looked around at her fellow debaters. Several were upperclassmen. She nodded and stood tall. "I'm ready."

The others studied her expression. When they saw she was calm, they seemed to calm themselves. Being the captain of the debate team, Mia felt it was her job to keep a cool head and rein in the others. By her actions, they followed suit. Mr. Harris, their advisor, approached and stared at his students. Not ten minutes before, they were all a bundle of nerves. Now, they all looked cool, calm, and collected. Like nothing would stop them.

"Ready?" he asked, not wanting to throw them off their game.

Mia nodded. Mr. Harris held the curtain back, and as they introduced the team, Mia led them out. Three hours later, Mia stood at her podium in stunned silence while waiting for the judges' results. Because of their wins this year, her school had hosted the debate. The other team had to drive in from Northern Idaho. If Mia and her team won this round, then they would head to Nationals and would represent Idaho as an entire state. A lot was riding on this decision.

"Ladies and Gentlemen," Mr. Harris called out as he approached the center of the stage. "If you'll take your seats, the judges have reached their decision." He held out his hand, and Mia noted that it was shaking. It took at least three tries to open the envelope, causing Mia's nerves to scream. Mr. Harris looked at the crowd, then at both teams. He drew in a deep breath and pulled the card from the envelope. "The winner of today's debate is..." Mia didn't hear the actual words come out of Mr. Harris' mouth, because her teammates were screaming, laughing, and crying all at once. Everyone grabbed Mia and hoisted her onto their shoulders. It took everything she had not to fall. She heard her name and looked out into the audience. Both her parents were fighting their way to her.

"Put me down!" she shouted, and as soon as her feet hit the floor, someone grabbed her and sandwiched her between her parents. Unable to grasp what had happened, Mr. Harris came up and hugged her too.

"Congratulations, Mia! You led your team to the state championship. The next stop is Nationals!" He hugged her again and twirled her around. When he set her down, Mia had to grab her father's arms to keep from face planting.

It was her mother that pushed her down to the floor, then shoved her head between her knees. After several minutes, Mia waved her hand, looked up at her parents, and grinned. "We won!"

"You did." Guthrie helped her to her feet and hugged her again. "We are so proud of you, Mia. We didn't want to distract you, but we arrived early and sat in the back." Her father hugged her again, then leaned in to whisper, "Are you sure you don't want to be a lawyer?"

Mia snorted a laugh. "Not on your life." She hugged her parents. "I don't know what I want to be when I grow up. I know it won't be a lawyer. And that's only because I've seen how much work you and grandpa put in. It's not for me. Whenever I decide I want to have a family, then I want to be comfortable either working from home or quitting my job. No offense, Dad, Mom, but I want to be there as my kids grow up."

Before they could say anything, Mia's teammates rushed up and asked if she wanted to join them in a celebration at the local pizza parlor. She looked at her parents, and it surprised her when they offered to go with them. The rest of that night set the precedent for the next two years. Guthrie and Midge Cunningham attended every one of Mia's debates, her volleyball games, and her softball games.

Two years later, when Mia left for the University of Buffalo on an academic scholarship, she left knowing that her parents really loved her, that she wasn't an inconvenience or an afterthought. In the two years before leaving for school, they had taught her how to cook, bake, and grill. Her father also taught her how to balance her checkbook and negotiate for a used car loan. She took him with her before leaving for college and used his strategy to purchase a used car to drive across the country. Mia left Idaho two weeks before she was due to go to school to take her time. She made the trip in five days. Before check-in, Mia drove to Niagara Falls and stayed on both sides. Thank goodness her mother insisted she update her passport before leaving. The day she moved onto campus would be a day that changed her life forever.

CHAPTER FOUR
EAGAN

Two Years Later

Eagan Davenport rolled his eyes at the other people sitting with him when his best friend Rochelle Mason called him a name he hated. No matter how many times he told her not to call him "Egghead" she ignored him. He'd developed the habit of not answering her when she called him that. Pissed her off, but that was too bad. Being called "Egghead" pissed him off. It seemed that whenever something upset Roc, everyone should be concerned right along with her. But if she upset anyone else, then she got in their face and told them to "Suck it up, Buttercup." He was seriously beginning to wonder if their friendship would last much longer. Since attending the same college for the last two years, Eagan realized Roc never took the blame for anything she did, or for any of the problems she caused. According to her, it was everyone else's fault, not hers. Back in high school, he never saw this side of her. It made him wonder if she had always been like this, or if it was something new since attending college.

"Hey, Egghead," Roc called for the fourth time. Before he could answer her, Eagan saw someone step in front of Roc.

"Excuse me, but why are you calling that man degrading names? It's obvious by his expression that he doesn't like it. Why are you so hostile toward him?"

"Oh my god, I love you," Eagan blurted out. "Will you marry me?" No one had ever stood up for him against Roc since coming here. In the past, whoever tried Roc would belittle so severely that they stopped hanging out with them. Eagan glanced around at their group of friends and grinned when he saw their expressions of shock. He took it to be at both him and the newcomer. He studied her as he rose to his feet, immediately liking what he saw. She was short. Compared to Roc's five-foot-nine-inch frame, this woman barely came to the older woman's shoulder.

Eagan had never seen her on campus before, so she must be new this year. He wondered how old she was. But if she was here at the college, she had to be at least eighteen, or damn close. That wasn't bad compared to his twenty years. He had already been attending for two years and had two left. This was his first day back on campus after the summer break. Eagan continued to study the woman, and smirked when she crossed her arms over her chest, pushing up her breasts. From his position to the side of her, he saw they would be perfect handfuls for him. Flexing his fingers, he gave a small laugh. The next thing that intrigued him was that she had her brown hair pulled up in a ponytail. She had the classic girl-next-door look, unlike his real next-door neighbor, Roc, who over the last two years had several cosmetic surgeries done. He hadn't seen her for the whole summer after high school graduation, because she and her mother had spent that time in LA. The next time he saw her was when she'd walked on campus here in Buffalo. He had thought she'd gone to LA to get ready to go to Berkley in the fall. But no, she'd had a boob job. In Eagan's humble opinion, Roc's new boobs looked like shit on her frame. Because they were friends, he never hesitated to tell her. He grinned when he remembered it had pissed her off, because she hadn't talked to him for two whole days.

Eagan jerked when someone nudged his shoulders. He glanced over at his friend, then followed his eyes to the newcomer. The girl was checking him out from head to foot. Eagan grinned when her eyes reached his.

"Sure, why not, but can we wait until after college at least?"

Assuming it was an answer to his impromptu question, Eagan laughed. "Absolutely. I'm done in two years. You?"

"Same. Today's my first day, but I'm only getting a two-year degree."

"In?" Eagan asked as he stepped forward and held out his hand. "Eagan Davenport."

"Mia Cunningham."

"Beautiful name for a beautiful woman," he said, and as soon as their hands touched, he felt a tingle run up his arm. By the expression on her face, she must have felt it too. With her hand still in his, he continued his conversation. "If this is your first day, do you need help carrying things to your room?"

"Are you offering?"

"I am."

"Sure, I have a few more things to carry up." Together they turned and walked away. Eagan froze when Rochelle screeched at him.

"What about me?"

Before Eagan could react, it amazed him when Mia turned and said, "What about you? This fine gentleman is helping me. From your actions earlier, you obviously don't care about him, so what about you?" When Roc continued to stand there stunned, Mia frowned then nodded her head. "Ah, you're one of those women, aren't you. It's all about you all the time. If you're not the center of attention, you're not happy. Sorry about your luck, Sweetie, but like I said, this fine gentleman is busy." She looked up at Eagan and grinned, but not before linking her elbow with his.

Eagan's next action seemed to startle them both. He reached down, grasped her jaw in both his hands, swooped down, and kissed her hard. It didn't take long for Mia to sigh against his lips, and he swooped in with his tongue to tangle with hers. They didn't break apart until Roc yelled at him.

"Eagan Michael Davenport! What the hell do you think you're doing? Are you going to allow this tramp to talk to me like this?"

Eagan broke off the kiss, sighed heavily, then put his forehead on Mia's, whispering, "I'm sorry." But he took a bracing breath, turned toward Roc, and threw his arm around Mia's shoulders, bringing her closer to him. Inside he was doing a happy dance when she placed one hand on his chest and wrapped her other arm around his waist. So together, they turned to face Roc as one.

"What do you want me to do, Roc? I've told you for the last twenty years that I hate being called 'Egghead.' Yet you insist on doing it. A total stranger stuck up for me. I like that. Since you never listen, maybe it's time for me to branch out and surround myself with people who have my best interests at heart. Not someone afraid to say anything because of your wrath. I'm tired of it. If you can't be nice to Mia, then don't hang around us. Because of what she did, I'm going to hang out with her and get to know her better." After that speech, he turned with Mia and walked away. For the first time in his life, he realized that maybe what his high-school girlfriend, Sue Ellen, had told him might be right.

"Where do you need help?" Eagan asked, still not removing his arm from around her shoulders.

"I'm parked over in the student parking," Mia said, as they walked in that direction.

Eagan frowned as he walked toward where she said her car was parked. "How did you end up in the quad if you're parked way over here?" He paused and turned in a circle to get his bearings. "Not that I'm ungrateful for you sticking up for me, but it's pretty far away."

"Yeah, I was taking a break from moving in. My roommate was saying goodbye to her boyfriend." She looked at him and raised her brows several times. Eagan laughed and hugged her. "I said I'd be back in an hour. I was on my way back when I heard that woman call you that name. By your expression, I could tell it upset you. Why did you let her get away with it?"

Eagan sighed, and instead of having his arm wrapped around her, he took her hand in his. "Roc and I go back, *way* back."

"Oh, are you former or current boyfriend and girlfriend?"

"Good God, no!" Eagan was so adamant about it, Mia immediately believed him. "No, we grew up in the same neighborhood. We lived directly across the street from each other. Though our birthdays are only one day apart, we are exactly twelve hours apart. I'm older. At the time, we were the only kids our age in the neighborhood, so we hung out together. It wasn't until we started kindergarten that we realized there were other kids our ages who lived around us. Roc, her real name is Rochelle, she's been my best friend since day one. I keep telling her the same thing over and over, but she won't take the hint."

When he remained silent, Mia asked, "What's that?"

Eagan exhaled, then stopped walking. He turned to her and, with his hands on her shoulders, said, "I have absolutely no romantic or sexual feelings toward her. None, even when we were younger, and you'd experiment, nothing. I never did that with her, absolutely no interest. Hell, I remember one time we were in Robert's basement playing spin the bottle. It was her turn to spin, and I was called away. She wouldn't shut up about it for a month. We were only twelve. That's when I first told her I thought of her as my sister, not a girlfriend, and that she would *never* be my girlfriend. She was pissed at me for a long time, but eventually came back around." He frowned and looked off into space.

"What?"

"I dated a girl for two years in high school. We both knew that we wouldn't continue dating after we graduated. I was okay with that. We wanted to concentrate on our careers. I knew I was coming here. She went to Harvard."

"And?"

"And she told me that Roc was in love with me. I never believed it. I didn't see Roc all summer after graduation. She and her mother rented a place in LA for the summer. Personally, I thought it was because she had been accepted to

Berkley, and they were getting ready for her to start school there. It shocked the hell out of me when she walked on campus here two days before classes started. She never told anyone she had even applied here, let alone been accepted." Eagan frowned, but Mia began to wonder. Finally, she shrugged and took Eagan's hand in hers as they headed toward her small SUV.

"Have you ever driven in snow before?"

"I have. Why?"

"Just wondering. I notice you have four-wheel drive. The winters around here can be brutal. Especially with the snow coming off the lake."

"That's why I bought it," Mia grinned as she opened the back and pointed to three boxes. "Those are the last of it." It impressed her when Eagan stacked the two largest on top of each other and lifted them.

"If you grab the last one, I'll follow you."

"Thanks." She did, then locked her car and slowly walked to her dorm. Outside her room, she set her box down and giggled. "I wonder if my roommate's boyfriend has left yet."

Eagan smirked as he reached up and pounded on the door. In less than a minute, it was whipped open by a man Mia had never seen before. The two stared at each other, then Eagan laughed.

"Davis? Davis Hollingsworth? What the hell are you doing here?"

The girl in the room turned from her bed and joined them, "Who are you?"

"Heather, this is Eagan Davenport. I went to high school with him. Eagan, how the hell are you? And what are you doing here?"

"I met Mia in the quad and offered to help her finish moving in. What are you doing here? Are you still in the Marines?"

"I am. This is my girlfriend, the one I told you about when I moved to your town for my senior year. We stayed in touch that year and for the last two while I was in the Marines. I was able to get leave to help her move in." The other man looked at Mia and grinned. "Thank you for giving us some time together."

"Not a problem. Thank you for serving." She offered her hand in a shake. Introductions were made, and Davis helped Eagan carry in the last three boxes.

"So, how long are you in town for?" Eagan asked the other man as he sat in the desk chair on Mia's side of the room.

"I'm here for a week."

"Where are you staying?"

"Don't know yet. I could drive back and forth to my grandparents, but I don't want to. I want to be as close to Heather as I can."

"Stay at my place," Eagan blurted out. "I don't live on campus. I have a one-bedroom about ten blocks from here. Depending on traffic, it takes fifteen to twenty minutes. And that's on a bad day." He looked over at Heather and smiled at the cute blonde. "If that's okay with you?"

"Yes!" Heather said and ran up to hug him. She turned to Davis. "If you want to, I don't want to pressure you."

"Pressure all you want, babe," Davis said. "If you're serious, then yes," Davis said to Eagan. "I can't thank you enough."

"Will you be at tonight's mixer?" Heather asked.

"What mixer?"

"It's a welcome party for the freshmen, but anyone can show up," Mia said, as she continued to unload some books onto a set of shelves, then break down the box. It surprised Eagan when she shoved it beneath her bed. At his frown, she giggled. "Never know when you're going to need it again."

"Are you going to the mixer?"

"I was planning on it for a couple of hours."

"If you're going, I'll go."

"Deal," Eagan said. He stood then kissed her. It was only their second kiss, but he couldn't get enough of her sweet taste. After he broke off, he looked at the others in the room. "Why don't I take Davis to my place, then we'll meet you back here in three hours. This way, you can finish unpacking and get ready. Where do you want to meet?"

"Back here," Davis said, as he looked around the room. "Don't hang any of your pictures until I can help," he said sternly to Heather. "Understand?"

"Yep." She laughed, then kissed him again before shoving him toward the door. "Three hours."

The men left, and on the way out of the dorm, Eagan shook his head. "I can't believe I ran into you. Such a small world. So, how're the Marines treating you?"

"Good," he said, then sighed. "I only got this leave because when I go back, I'm being deployed to Afghanistan for thirteen months. I haven't told Heather yet."

"Oh, man, that's rough. I'm sure she'll understand. If she waited for you all this time, I'm sure she'll wait for you until you get back."

"I hope so. There were a few rocky months there when I first moved in with my grandparents, but I'm sure we can survive this." He sighed and followed Eagan to the parking lot. Thirty minutes later, they were walking into Eagan's apartment. Eagan stopped dead and demanded.

"What the fuck are you doing here? I never gave you a key." He stepped aside, and Davis stared in shock at the woman standing there. It took a brief moment to realize it was Rochelle Mason. She'd had a boob job, her nose looked different, as did her eyes, and her lips looked like a thousand hornets had stung her. Her new 'looks' were awful.

"Yes, you did," Roc said.

"No, I didn't." Eagan held out his hand. "I would have remembered. Give it back." When he received it, he turned and handed it to Davis. "Here, this way, you can come and go. You won't have to wait for me."

"Why does he get a key, and who the hell is he?" Rochelle howled at Eagan.

"Hello, Rochelle," Davis said. He gave her a small wave. "Davis Hollingsworth."

"From senior year? What are you doing here?"

"His girlfriend checked in today. I saw him, and he's here for another week. I offered him a place to stay." He looked at Davis and winced. "Sorry, but it's only a couch."

"Not a problem. I've slept on worse."

"He can't stay here," Rochelle screeched.

Eagan paused, crossed his arms over his impressive chest, and glared at his best friend. "You better tread lightly here, Roc. You're about five minutes away from being kicked out of my life. Tell me, why can't *I* invite a friend to stay in *my* apartment?"

"We were going to watch movies tonight."

"No, you wanted to watch movies tonight. I hadn't decided what I was going to do. You interrupted my conversation with the others, then Mia arrived. For your information, I have a date. Now, please leave." Eagan walked over to the front door and opened it. He never said another word until she walked by. Unfortunately, Rochelle got the last word in, and her statement made him shudder.

"That fucking cunt bitch will fucking regret taking what's mine."

As soon as she left, Eagan shut the door and turned to Davis. "Sorry about that."

"No problem. I see things haven't changed."

"What's that mean?"

"It means she's still in love with you. I saw it in high school."

"Naw, that's not it."

"Whatever, man. Don't say I didn't warn you. Someday that controlling bitch is going to snap, and you'll be left wondering what the fuck happened."

Eagan stared at his friend in confusion. Instead of asking more questions, he gave Davis the five-second tour. They caught up as they got ready for their dates.

CHAPTER FIVE
ROCHELLE

Rochelle stormed out of Eagan's apartment, so pissed she had to stop to catch her breath. Her entire body shook from her anger. "How fucking dare he treat me like that?" She growled beneath her breath. Roc straightened to her full height and strode down the hallway with her head held high. She'd get back at both of them, *just watch and see*. But first, she had to do some research.

While Rochelle didn't live on campus, she didn't live in the same neighborhood as Eagan did either. Ten minutes after leaving Eagan's apartment, she walked into her own. She knew it wasn't as fabulous as she deserved, but she had to settle for what her father would dole out in his paltry allowance. Who allowed their only daughter to live on five thousand dollars a month? It was outrageous the things she'd had to give up since attending college here. Heaving a frustrated sigh, Roc grabbed her laptop, sat at her dining room table, and fired it up. Before she got down to business, she poured herself a glass of wine, grabbed a pad of paper and a pen. She downed the first glass in only four swallows and had to refill it before she could begin.

As she fired up her laptop, she paused, swearing. "Fuck, what was that cunt's name?" She sat back and rubbed her forehead, trying to think. The only name that came to her was Bea. Her research was getting her nowhere.

Her next step was to access the University's website to see if she could hack into their database. No such luck. Something caught her eye, and she read it twice before she realized what she was reading. Thinking back to the first encounter with the cunt, Roc finished her second glass and poured herself a third. As she sat and stared at her computer, she plotted how to get even with the cunt. No one, and she meant no one breathing, would ever come between her and Eagan. How dared she do it? And what the fuck was up with Eagan. He'd stood there and laughed. Then he had the audacity to kiss the cunt in front of her. Never had she been so humiliated in her life. She picked up her phone and began calling her friends. By the sixth person and her fourth glass of wine, she finally realized no one was picking up her calls.

Rochelle jumped to her feet to pace. How in the fuck could she seek her revenge if no one answered their damn phone to help her? Incensed, she poured herself yet another glass of wine. Realizing it was empty, she threw the empty bottle against the far wall and reached for the next one. Seeing there was none left, she grabbed her keys and headed out. Knowing she was too drunk to drive, and also understanding there was a liquor store only two blocks from her apartment, Rochelle set out on foot. Thirty minutes later, she was back with four bottles of wine. Not that she would need that much, but she had a feeling she would need it in the coming weeks. Thank god she was twenty-one, and her father couldn't question her purchases on the credit card he paid for.

All the way to the liquor store, Rochelle had recalled what that cunt had said to her. All the wine she ever bought came sealed with a cork. At the last minute, on her way out the door, she bought a bottle with a screw-cap. The closer to her apartment, the more she fumed, the more she drank. By the time she arrived home, she had finished that one bottle. Pouring another glass, she paced her apartment. Looking at her laptop screen again, she realized the cunt would go to the mixer that night. It seemed like the thing something that small-minded would do. Deciding, Roc stormed to her bedroom to get ready. As soon as she entered the bedroom, she tripped over the pile of clothes on the floor, landed half off, and half on the bed, swearing as she went down, and banging her knee on the footboard of the bed.

ROCHELLE WOKE WITH the worst headache of her life. She looked around and couldn't remember how she had ended up on the floor. Sitting up, she frowned at the mess at the foot of her bed before she noticed a glass of wine had spilled. Screeching, she jumped to her feet, rushed into the bathroom, and grabbed a rag to run under cold water. She usually wouldn't bother with the stain, but she'd fired her housekeeper three days ago, and somehow a glass of red wine had landed on a pure white carpet.

Bent over the mess, she scrubbed as hard as she could. Grabbing her phone, she called Eagan to see if he could help her. It was bad enough she was going to have to pay for the repairs on the walls. It wasn't her fault people pissed her off, and she threw things. She knew Eagan would come to her rescue. When she only got voicemail, Roc sat back on her heels and screamed into the bedding.

"Son of a fucking bitch! How dare he ignore me!" She fumed and threw her phone. She screamed harder when it hit the brick of the fireplace and shattered. "Who the fuck puts a fireplace in the bedroom, anyway." She shook her head, sat back on her heels, and cried.

"This is all that cunt's fault. If it hadn't been for her, Eagan and I would have been watching movies last night. Now, because of her, Eagan yelled at me. My friends are ignoring me. Eagan took the key I copied from his ring away from me. This is all that cunt's fault. I'll teach them. I'll ignore Eagan for a week. See if he doesn't come crawling back to me. I'll make him suffer until he sees the error of his ways. Then, when he's on his knees crawling back to me, I'll take him back. But only then." With that plan said out loud, Roc did the best she could to clean up her mess. It was a Sunday, and she checked the website to see if the store for her phone was open. After spending almost three hours in the shower and getting ready, she drove to the store to replace her phone.

Unfortunately, they didn't have the phone she wanted. She wanted to upgrade to the newest edition of her current phone. After being told she had to wait for at least two weeks, she stormed out. On the way back to her apartment, she made a quick stop at the grocery store. Not that she cooked, but she was running low on microwaveable meals.

If her housekeeper had done her job and cleaned up after Roc, then she wouldn't be in this predicament. How dare the shrew ask for more money when Rochelle told her to cook? It was part of her fucking job. Who gave a damn that cooking wasn't in the original contract? The bitch was getting paid good money to work for Roc. She should have been honored for the privilege, but no, she had to demand more money. That was when Rochelle fired her raggedy ass. Now she had to do it all herself. The injustice of it was unfathomable to Roc.

Once Roc returned home, she put away her groceries, and because none of the people she had contacted last night or this morning answered her calls, and she couldn't call anyone because she still didn't have a phone, she cleaned her apartment. Five hours later, she slammed her laptop case down in frustration. She had started to pick up her space, but found it too hard to do. Because she didn't have a phone, she'd e-mailed her father asking for his help. It took several e-mails for Rochelle to tell her father about all the problems she had and what that cunt had done to her. However, she didn't use that word to her father. In a nutshell, her father acted like a bastard. He said he would pay for a new phone when it came in, but as for her request for a housekeeper, she was on her own.

After reminding her he knew of no twenty-one-year-old college students who had a housekeeper, a cook, or maid, and if she wanted one, she had two choices. One, pay for them herself, or two, move to California and live with them. After Rochelle had left for college, her parents had packed up and moved lock, stock, and barrel to Los Angeles. Her father had taken a job there and hadn't consulted with Roc about the move. Now, not only was he telling her to hire her own housekeeper or cook, he'd just informed her if she didn't stop her useless spending on clothes, he would cancel her credit card. That was when she slammed the laptop shut.

"This is all that cunt's fault. If she hadn't shown up, none of this would have happened." Rochelle fumed. The longer she sat and thought about it, the more she planned her revenge. She didn't know when, she didn't know how, but she would get that cunt back if it was the last thing she did. No one took her man from her. No one!

FOUR DAYS LATER, CLASSES started for the new semester. Rochelle sat in her usual seat in her first class and looked about. This professor allowed the students to sit where they liked. In the past, she and Eagan had always sat together. But today, he wasn't there. It wasn't until lunchtime that she realized why her man hadn't been in any of her classes. They had been in the same ones for the last two years, because their majors overlapped. Eagan was enrolled in the Criminology program, while Roc enrolled in Law. The realization she probably wouldn't see him during the day pissed her off even more.

That night, Roc went home and mapped out her schedule. Instead of going to the law library during her free time, she would stalk the Criminology department to see if she could run into Eagan. If that cunt was with him, Rochelle didn't know what she would do. With a firm plan in place, she finally buckled down to do her homework— the first time for everything. Not wanting to admit the work was hard and that she'd slept with several teacher's assistants to get a passing grade, she realized if she didn't want to flunk, she'd better start doing the work herself.

Things started looking up for her when she stopped by the phone company and received her new upgraded phone. The icing on the cake, they could retrieve her SIM card from her last phone, and she didn't lose any numbers. The first person she called was Eagan. She left him a message she had been out of touch, because her phone had broken. No way was she going to tell him it died because of her. He didn't need to know that. Again, after all this time, she left a voicemail. She couldn't understand why he didn't answer her call on the first ring. It wasn't like she wasn't the most important person in his life.

Rochelle never laid eyes on Eagan again until the week of mid-terms, when they were all getting ready to head home for the Thanksgiving holiday. She saw him across the quad and trudged through the un-shoveled sidewalks. She didn't see who he was with until she jumped on his back, reached around, and kissed his cheek.

"It's been so long. Why haven't you answered any of my calls?" She reprimanded him, and when he turned and glared at her, she quickly hopped down and felt ashamed for her actions. Not liking that feeling one bit, she crossed her arms and glared at him. "Well? Are you going to answer my questions?"

"I don't answer to you," Eagan said coldly. "If you must know, I've been busy with my classes and with Mia. What is so important that you're interrupting us this time?"

Eagan's tone of voice shocked Roc, and as she looked around at their friends, she saw they glared at her too. "What the fuck is up with everyone? Why are you all pissed at me? I did nothing."

When everyone stared at her in shock, she took two steps back, then another two when Eagan leaned down and got into her face. He was livid. Not once in all their lives had Roc ever seen him this pissed. "Did you or did you not post on the campus website the night of the welcome mixer that Mia was a whore, and she slept with anyone with a dick between their legs?"

"What? No, I didn't."

"Yes, you did." A girl Roc had never met before pushed her way between them. She held up her phone and showed her. "I could access the web address of the post, and it came back to you. What is your problem with Mia? She is the sweetest, most caring, and most loving person you could ever have the privilege to meet. What you did was horrible. I can only hope karma comes back and bites you in the ass."

"But, Eagan." Rochelle held her hand out toward him, but he ignored it.

"I don't want to hear it, Rochelle," he began. Hearing her actual name from his lips was like a punch to the gut. He never called her by her birth name unless he was distraught with her. Roc could remember only twice in the past he had used it. "Sue Ellen told me of your obsession with me back in high school. I never believed her. Then Davis told me the same thing when we found you in my apartment."

"She was in your apartment?" Mia asked.

"You have no say in this, Bitch," Roc growled.

"Yes, she does. I'm dating her, and we are exclusive. Tomorrow, after Mia's last class, she's going home with me for the Thanksgiving holiday to meet Mom and Dad. You are not invited. Go to California to visit your parents." Eagan turned his back on her, then whipped back around. "Maybe you should think about staying there and going to Berkley like you originally planned. I know I don't want you around here." This time when he turned his back on her, he wrapped an arm around Mia, and everyone in the group, all twelve people, turned and walked away from her.

Several minutes later, Roc looked up and glared at their retreating backs. "I'll get you back for this, you cunt. No one humiliates me like this and gets away with it. Payback is a bitch, and I'm the biggest and worst one you'll ever encounter. Count on it, you fucking cunt." With her head held high, Roc turned on her heel and went to her next class. It would be months before she realized that she actually had posted that on the campus website. In her defense, it was the night everyone had met Mia, and Roc had been so drunk she didn't know what she was doing.

CHAPTER SIX
MIA

Mia shut the door behind her, leaned against it, and hugged herself. She looked over at her roommate, Heather, and said, "Oh, my god!"

"What? Your boyfriend is totally sexy. How long have you been dating?"

Mia giggled as she looked at her watch, then grinned. "Twenty minutes."

Heather had been unpacking a box. At Mia's answer, she turned to gawk at her. *"WHAT?"*

"When you asked me to give you an hour to say goodbye, I walked around campus." Mia began, then stood and went over to unpack her own boxes. They both worked at putting their room together as Mia explained what had happened.

Heather sat on her bed and stared at Mia in shock. "Let me get this straight. You heard someone call. What was his name again?"

"Eagan."

"Okay, you heard a woman call Eagan, Egghead, and you yelled at her? Why would you do that?"

Mia shrugged, then sighed as she sat on her bed. "I don't know. I think it was a combination of things. I may be only eighteen, but all my life, I always fought for the underdog.

Whenever I saw someone being bullied or picked on, I couldn't help myself. I would jump in with both feet to protect them. Did it this time too, but it was his expression, along with the people they were around. Eagan kept rolling his eyes like he'd heard it before. I didn't jump into the fray until I heard him tell her not to call him by that name. She wouldn't stop. That's when I got in her face."

"How?"

"I yelled at her. Asked her why she was a bully." Mia giggled and flopped back on her bed. Two seconds later, she popped back up and laughed. "Before I finished berating the woman, who is Eagan's best friend, he said he loved me and asked me to marry him."

"Oh my god, what did you say?" Heather giggled.

"I looked him up and down, shrugged, then said, 'Sure, but can we wait until after we finish college first?' He agreed. Then he shocked me when he ignored Roc, that's the chick's name, threw his arm around my shoulders, and asked if I needed help to move in. When we walked away, this chick demanded he stay with her. He ignored her. I don't really recall what happened, but I repeated something. Next thing I know, he's kissing me."

"Oh, wow." Heather sat there in stunned silence. After studying her roommate, she frowned. "Why are you freaked out?"

"Because that was my first kiss ever. Then the second kiss was when he left here with your boyfriend. I'm sorry, but I don't remember his name."

"Davis. Davis Hollingsworth. And no, he's not as rich as his name sounds. He's two years older than me. During his junior and senior years, his father, who is in the Marines, transferred to Japan for two years. Davis has two younger brothers and a younger sister. They are several years younger. Not wanting to leave in his senior year, he moved in with his grandparents. Unfortunately, he wasn't able to finish high school with the same people he'd been with the last four years."

"What's that mean?" Mia asked, as she continued to organize her side of the room.

"If you can't tell from my accent, I'm from Virginia. Davis's father worked at Quantico for four years. He, General Hollingsworth, is career military. They lived off base, and in the small town we lived in, there was only one school that held all the grades."

"I understand. I come from the same size. Different floors." At Heather's frown, she elaborated. "The first floor was for kindergarten to third grade. The second floor was fourth through sixth. Then the top two floors were for the junior and senior high."

"Okay, but we only had one level, they spread out our school, and the different grades were in different wings."

"Ah, okay, continue."

"Oh, Davis was in the eighth grade when he started at my school. I was in the sixth. So I didn't see him until I moved over to that wing a year later. His siblings were even younger than me. There is a seven-year gap from Davis to the next sibling, then they're like a year apart." Heather giggled. "The general was stationed overseas after Davis was born."

"And his mom was here?"

"Yep. Anyway, I was in the eighth grade when I realized Davis lived only four houses down from mine. I was sitting outside reading one day, and he came up and introduced himself. I was such a bookworm, I never really paid attention to my neighbors. When I met Davis, I finally took my nose out of a book. We had fun that summer. Even though he was two years older, it didn't seem like such a stretch. Anyway, then the general transferred yet again, only this time Davis refused to move. He wanted to finish high school in the States. Unfortunately, his father would only agree if he went to live with his grandparents. His mother's parents. That's where he met your Eagan." Heather sighed and stopped hanging her clothes in the closet to look over at her roommate. "I didn't see much of Davis after that. Though we talked every day and sent e-mails. The first time I saw him after he left was when my parents drove me here to go to his senior prom."

"Wow, your parents did that for you?"

"Yeah, only because I had been interested in this school for like ever, and they thought it would be a good idea to check out the area. So they brought me up for the weekend. I saw Davis again six weeks later when he graduated. Afterward, he returned to Virginia and stayed with us until he had to leave for the Marines. That happened in the middle of August. I saw him again after boot camp, but today is the first time in almost two years since I've seen him. We still write or talk almost every day. I only wish..." She let the sentence hang in the air.

"Wish?" Mia prompted after several moments of silence.

"I only wish he wouldn't get deployed overseas. I know he must, but still, it's my greatest fear."

"Oh, wow."

"Yeah." The two girls remained silent as they finished organizing their room. Exhausted, they looked at each other and grinned.

"First dibs on the shower," Mia said as she jumped to her feet, scooped up her toiletries she hadn't taken into the bathroom yet, and hurried past Heather. The room she had requested and been assigned had its own bathroom. Though she knew her parents could afford it for herself, she had opted to request a roommate. As she showered, she thought back to the events of the day and did a happy dance when she realized that life was beautiful, and she couldn't wait to see what the night would bring.

"READY?" EAGAN LOOKED at Davis after he parked his car next to Mia's. He had the parking sticker on his car window, so he could park anywhere on campus. The two men had discussed leaving Davis's rental in the lot at Eagan's apartment and returning to the campus in his car. Tonight's mixer was for new and returning students, along with the faculty, and any parents, siblings, or significant others, husbands, or wives, that wanted to attend. The only time, besides graduation and open house, that many people were invited on campus.

"I guess," Davis said, as he leaned forward and looked out the windshield. He glanced back at his friend and sighed. "What is this thing, anyway?"

"A mixer. It's really for the incoming freshmen, but open to all students enrolled here at UB. I went to my first one, but not the next year. Not that I'm a snob, but it's not really my cup of tea."

"So, what do you do?"

"The students get to mingle with the faculty. Tables will be set up from the different sororities and fraternities trying to recruit new members."

"Do you belong to a frat house?"

"No, never had an interest in stuff like that. What about you?"

"Actually, the Marines are like that. I'll probably never have the college experience."

"Why do you say that?"

"Because though I love being a Marine and plan to be in at least ten years, I've already started taking online classes. I've completed a year of college already. I take the classes in my downtime from being a marine, which isn't a lot of time, but I'm making it work." They sat there for several minutes in silence, then Davis pulled his phone and looked at Eagan.

"Stupid question. Can we exchange numbers? Being a marine brat, I don't have a lot of close childhood friends. I've always liked you, Eagan."

"Thank you, I liked you too." Eagan grinned as he pulled out his phone, and they exchanged numbers and e-mail addresses. Eagan sighed, then murmured, "Do you want me to keep tabs on Heather for you?"

"No, I trust her," he said it with such conviction that Eagan believed him. He looked at the clock on the dash and said it was time to go. Together, the two men exited Eagan's SUV and made their way to the dorms. Their knock was answered in seconds.

"Hey," Eagan said to Mia when she opened the door.

"Hey," she smiled, and stood on tiptoes and kissed the corner of his mouth. "We're ready."

"Let's go." Eagan stepped back and laughed when Davis pushed him aside to get to Heather. The couple greeted each other in the room's privacy, before joining the other couple in the hall.

"So, what's supposed to happen tonight?" Mia asked, as Eagan twined his fingers with hers.

"Like it says, a mixer, a mixture of students, faculty, family members. You mix and mingle. There will be tables from the different sororities and fraternities trying to recruit new members."

"Yuck," both Heather and Mia spoke as one.

"You don't want to join a sorority?" Davis asked.

"Why? I don't really want girls with over-inflated egos telling me what to do. I'm not here for that. I'm here to get an education," Mia said.

"Me, too," Heather spoke. "You remember me being a bookworm? I want to study and get good grades. Why should I have other girls that are all about the social connection tell me what to do? I'm not interested."

"Oh." Both men didn't know what else to say.

"Are you in a fraternity?" Mia asked Eagan.

"No, like you, I want to get an education. I'll be honest, I go to the parties, and some of my friends belong, but it's not for me."

"What's your major?" Heather asked.

"Criminology. I want the degree before I decide whether I want to be a cop or an FBI agent."

"You could always join the marines," Davis spoke. "That's the degree I'm doing online."

They talked about the merits of joining the service on their way to the mixer. The two couples spent several hours there, and when they left, they had several invitations to join different sororities, which the girls politely refused. Both had several t-shirts with the name of the university on them. With very little persuading, Mia went home with Eagan, while Davis stayed in the dorm room with Heather.

"I LIKE THIS," MIA SAID, as she walked into Eagan's apartment. She strolled around, and from the other side of the room, turned to look at him.

"What?"

"I've done nothing like this before. You make me lose my senses when you're so close." She laughed. "Not that it's bad, but I can't think when we touch."

"And this is a bad thing?"

"No, it's just that the kiss you planted on me in the quad was my first-ever kiss."

"What? No way, I'm sure you left a string of broken hearts back home."

"Nope, you're the first. I had no interest in dating. Well, I did, but it seemed like the boys I was interested in didn't have any interest in me."

"Do you know why? Because from where I'm standing, you are one beautiful girl."

"Could be my mouth." Mia waved her hand when she said it, then after realizing what she said, she slapped a hand over it. "I didn't mean that."

Laughing, Eagan came closer, took her hand, and pulled her down onto his couch. "I know, but what did you mean?"

"I told this to Heather earlier, but I always fight for the underdog. That's why I did what I did in the quad. Your facial expression said it upset you with how that chick talked to you. Maybe it was because I was the captain of the debate team, or just my personality, but I needed to say something."

"I'm glad you did. Now we are together," Eagan said, and pulled her into his arms. His phone rang, but after seeing the number, he turned it off. "It was her."

"Are you sure I'm not coming between the two of you?"

"I'm sure." Then he swooped in and kissed her. Several minutes later, with them both breathing hard, Eagan placed his forehead on hers. "As much as I want to strip you naked and take you to my room, we'd better stop." When she said nothing, he continued. "I don't have any condoms." He paused, then whispered, "I'm staking my claim on you. I want you, Mia. Not only sexually, but I'd like to date you. We can take the sex part slow. I promise not to push you until you are ready."

"Ah, and I'm not on any birth control." She paused, then sighed. "And I like that you want to claim me. Makes me feel special. If you're sure we can take it slow, then I would like to date you, too." They ended up making popcorn and watching a movie. They fell asleep, stretched out on the couch, wrapped in each other's arms.

EAGAN AND MIA JERKED awake at the pounding on the apartment door. Mia fell off the couch as Eagan reared up. Before either of them could do anything, the door whipped open, and Heather and Davis rushed inside.

"What's wrong?" Eagan frowned at their frantic expressions.

"I think I nipped it in the bud," Heather began, "But we might have a problem."

"What's that?" Mia asked, as she rose from the floor.

Heather looked around, then spotted the small kitchen island. She whipped out her laptop, and her finger flew over the keyboard. While she did that, Eagan looked at Davis.

"What's going on?"

"Not exactly sure, but someone knocked on Heather's door this morning and showed her something. They talked, and she demanded I bring her here. No clue what's going on?"

"Eagan, do you know a Rochelle Mason?" Heather asked, from her location on the other side of the room.

"Yes, Davis does too. We went to high school together, and she's my best friend."

"That's the chick I told you about," Mia said, as she helped herself to look through Eagan's cupboards to make coffee.

"Shit," Heather said. When the coffee finished, everyone sat around. Heather spoke. "The guy that knocked on our door was a guy I've been talking to since being accepted at UB. He's taking the same courses I am. We're enrolled in the computer science program. In a nutshell, we know computers inside and out. We write code. He knocked on my door, because he's super shy and didn't go to the mixer last night. But he watched it through a live feed and where other students posted comments and pictures."

"Okay," the others said, understanding what she was saying.

"Gregory, that's what he prefers to be called, saw a post. He could stop it, but he wanted me to be aware of what was happening."

"And what is happening?" Mia frowned at her roommate.

Heather turned her computer to show them a message in her e-mail. "Gregory deleted it from the campus website, but not until this morning. He has no idea how many people saw it. He sent it to my e-mail, because I told him who my roommate was before I even moved here."

"Oh my god," Mia said, after reading it. She turned to Eagan in shock. Eagan leaned forward and swore.

"Son of a fucking bitch! She's gone too far this time."

"What?" Davis asked, as he leaned in and read it. He whistled and swore at the same time. Looking at Eagan, he asked, "What are you going to do?"

"Don't confront her," Mia begged. "If what I did yesterday causes this much backlash, I don't want you to confront her."

"Fine, I won't, but I can block her number and delete her from my e-mail contacts. I'll ignore her. Once Davis leaves, I'll have the locks on my apartment changed."

"Why would you wait until I leave? Do it now."

"Why would you do it in the first place?" Heather asked.

"Because when Davis and I came back here yesterday, Roc stood in this very room waiting for me. I never gave her a key to my apartment, but somehow she got one."

"Damn," they all said, and stared at the computer screen to read the message there.

If Gregory could be trusted, then the message posted all over the campus website stated: *Bea Cuntingham is a whore. Ladies, watch your man, because she will steal him right out from under your nose. This cunt needs to be stopped!* Then a fuzzy photo of Mia was attached.

"How do you know for sure it came from Roc?" Eagan asked.

"Because both Gregory and I could backtrack to the user, and it came back to a Rochelle Mason."

"Damn," Eagan said, and rubbed his face. He looked at Mia. "I'm so sorry."

"Don't be. As long as we're together, we can do this."

"I agree." He gathered her to him and kissed her hard. When they broke apart, he looked at the other couple and grinned. "I've staked my claim on Mia, so Roc can burn in hell for all I care."

It took some time, but Eagan got over Roc and focused all his attention on his studies and Mia. On the weekends, she stayed with him in his apartment, and though they hadn't consummated their relationship yet, they settled in like a couple who had been together for a long time. It wasn't until a few days before Thanksgiving break that either of them saw Roc again. It was a surprise, because everyone was in the quad, enjoying the mild weather, when out of the blue, someone jumped onto Eagan's back and kissed his face. Eagan stiffened and shrugged the person off. He whipped around and saw Roc standing there with a massive grin on his face. His first instinct was to protect Mia. With his arm wrapped around his girlfriend, he glared at her former friend.

"What the fuck do you think you're doing?"

Unfazed by his tone, she laughed. "God, Egghead, I've had such a shitty year so far. It's good to finally see you. What have you been up to?" She stepped forward to put her hand on his chest, but he jerked back.

"I have nothing to say to you," he said coldly, as Heather got into her face and shoved her phone into Roc's face, yelling at her. With his arm around Mia, he turned them both and walked away. "I'm sorry."

"Don't be," Mia said, as she looked over her shoulder and saw Roc storm away, but not before throwing a nasty glare Mia's way. The look on the other woman's face caused Mia to shudder.

"You okay?" Eagan asked as he felt her shake.

"Yeah, are you sure you should have been that mean to her? She seems pissed."

"I don't care. Rochelle has gone too far this time. I will not tolerate her spreading lies about you."

Mia sighed as Eagan wrapped both arms around her and gave her a gentle kiss. All was right in her world when he did that. If Mia had seen the expression on Roc's face at that moment, she would have done things differently.

CHAPTER SEVEN
EAGAN

Thirteen months later

Eagan rolled over and grinned when he saw Mia lying next to him in his bed. Since returning to school four months ago, Mia stayed with him at his apartment on the weekends. They still hadn't consummated their relationship, and Eagan was okay with that. Something about Mia made Eagan want to protect her at all costs. Though they hadn't had actual penetrative sex, they had enjoyed oral sex with one another. When she'd explained her reasoning, Eagan had agreed with her. She wanted to wait until their wedding night to go all the way. What they had at the moment was perfect for them.

Tomorrow they were both leaving to go home for the Christmas holiday. Unfortunately, they weren't able to go to each other's homes yet. Things had happened, and their schedules didn't mesh. Last fall Mia was supposed to go home with him for the Thanksgiving vacation, but her mother had called at the last minute and asked her to come home. Her father had experienced a small heart attack, and they wanted Mia home for the holiday. There was no way for them to say no.

Over the summer, Eagan had flown to California, and had a long conversation with Rochelle. He told her everything he thought he had in the past. How he had no sexual or romantic feelings for her. After finding out what she had done on the website, it took Eagan a long time to forgive her. It was Mia who asked him to patch things up with her. She understood what their friendship meant to each other and didn't want to be the one to cause the split between them.

"As long as she understands that you are not romantically interested in her," Mia told him. "I have no problem if she hangs out with us, but she needs to understand that I'm your girlfriend, not her. She's regulated to best friend, and that is all."

Eagan had agreed, and while on summer break, he'd gone to talk to Rochelle. It surprised him how much she agreed. She'd even told him she didn't care he didn't have romantic feelings for her, as long as she could be in his life. They had hung out for a week before Eagan left for home. His entire time in California, he'd talked to Mia. During one conversation, he even had her on speakerphone, so she understood exactly what he'd told Roc. Everyone was happy.

When the new semester started in August, Roc and Mia didn't welcome each other with open arms, but they were cordial to one another. Eagan sighed as he rose from the bed. After using the bathroom, he went to pour two cups of coffee. Luckily, they had fixed it the night before. There was one thing he needed to do before they left for the Christmas break. Because both he and Mia had a ton of stuff to do in their last semester when they returned. With both cups in his hands, he went back into the bedroom, put the cups on the nightstand, and crawled back into bed. Before turning to wake Mia, Eagan reached into the drawer to withdraw her Christmas gift. They had told each other not to exchange gifts, but he knew she would forgive him when she received hers. At least he hoped she would.

"Mia," Eagan whispered as he settled beneath the covers. Usually, she was the first one up, but she had worked well after midnight to turn in her paper last night. Tomorrow was the cut-off, but she had finished it and crashed when her head hit the pillow. It was now eight in the morning, and they both had last-minute things to do before heading home the next day.

"Mia, sweetie, it's eight in the morning, time to get up."

"Humph…" came the muffled reply. Eagan grinned when he saw her lying on her stomach, her head beneath the pillow, and her hair all over the place. Reaching up to rub her back, he grinned when she arched into it. He loved that her hair always covered her face. His biggest joy was moving it and running his fingers through its silkiness.

"Time to get up."

"I heard you the first time," she groused, but rolled over and only cracked one eye open. "Is the coffee done?"

"Yep, I have your cup over here." He pointed over his shoulder and laughed when she lurched up and demanded.

"Where?"

Laughing, he took her hands in his. "In a minute. I have to do something first."

"Eagan," Mia scolded him.

"It's all good." Eagan hopped up onto his knees and faced her. "Okay, I know this is sudden, and I know we said we would not exchange gifts. But I got you something."

"Eagan." Mia shook her head. He was always trying to spoil her.

"You'll like this, I promise," Eagan said, then reached beneath his pillow and pulled out the dark-blue velvet box. "Mia Cunningham, I love you. I asked you a year and a half ago to marry me. You said yes after we graduate. When we come back in January, we have five months of school left. I love you and want to marry you a month after graduation. Will you marry me?" He opened the box, then held it out for her to inspect the emerald and diamond ring.

"Yes!" Mia launched herself at him. They ended up tangled in the bed covers, kissing before he could get the ring on her finger. He sighed in relief when it was a perfect fit. After they sat back up, they shared their coffee.

"I wanted you to have this before you went home for the holidays. But, I want to ask your opinion about something."

"What's that?" Mia couldn't take her eyes off the ring on her left hand.

"Would you mind if I ask Roc to be my best woman?"

"As long as she knows you're marrying me and not her, I have no problem with it."

"Okay, I'll ask her when we get back. I know it's not a lot of time to plan a wedding, but I thought you could talk to your mother over the break, but I have to warn you."

"What's that?"

"I'll help with whatever I can, I'd like to get married here, so when you have a spare minute during the last semester, we can pick out the flowers, the cake, the venue. I'm sure my mom would help."

"What about you?"

"Yes, I'll help whenever I have time, but remember, I not only have a full class schedule, I also have the internship at the

Buffalo field office of the FBI. I don't know when I'll be able to help."

"Okay, I understand." She paused, looking at the ring, then looked him directly in the eye. "I'd like a small ceremony. Nothing over twenty people."

"That's doable, if later in the summer, if you agree, I can have my parents plan a gigantic reception."

"How gigantic are we talking?"

Eagan shrugged, then smirked. "Couple hundred people."

"Sounds like a plan. I'll talk to my mom over the holidays. With your permission, I'd like to give Mom your mother's contact information."

"Absolutely. Let's make sure you have it." They grabbed their phones and entered the information. They could spend the next hour together before Eagan had to rush off to his last class, and Mia had to go back to her dorm room to pack for her trip home. She ended up filling two extra suitcases to take her things home with her. Instead of driving, like she had when she'd arrived here, she had opted to fly. It was quicker and saved a lot of time. With the things she was taking back with her, it would give her less to pack when she finished school. She still didn't know what she wanted to do, but she knew that wherever Eagan was, she'd be happy. She couldn't wait to get back after the new year.

EAGAN SMILED AS HE hung up the phone with Mia. Currently, she was stuck in an airport in Chicago. They had delayed her connecting flight. He loved that she had updated him on her progress on her trip home. He only lived an hour and a half south of the University, so the drive hadn't been a hardship. He couldn't imagine trying to fly and miss a connecting flight.

Pulling into his space at his apartment, it didn't take long for him to unload his truck. With only one suitcase, he was unloaded and unpacked in under an hour of arriving home. Knowing that Mia wouldn't be in until the next day, he flopped on the couch, then grabbed his phone and made a call.

"Hello,"

"Roc, it's Eagan. What are you doing?"

"Nothing. I got back from California yesterday. What are you doing?"

"I just got back. I'm at my apartment. Want to come over?"

"Is Mia there?"

"Not at the moment. They delayed her flight. She's stuck at O'Hare until tomorrow."

"Wow, that sucks."

"Yeah, come over. We can order a pizza."

"Sure." They hung up, and two hours later, Roc arrived. Eagan frowned when he noticed that her hair, makeup, and clothes were perfect. Shaking his head, he closed the door. Only to take three steps and open it again at the knock. It was the pizza deliveryman. Paying for it, they filled a plate and settled on the couch. There was a long-running cop show on the TV. After eating two slices of the pie, Eagan muted the TV, turned to Roc, and drew in a deep breath. Letting it out slowly.

"I'd like to ask you a question."

"Sure, what's up?"

"Before the holiday, I asked Mia to marry me. She said yes. Would you be my best woman?" He studied his best friend, and frowned when she paled. He became worried when she said nothing for quite some time.

"Roc?"

"Oh, yeah, sorry. I was wondering how the wedding would work with you both having a semester left of school."

"We're getting married a month after graduation. Mom's been talking to Mia's mother over the holiday. The actual ceremony will be small, with about twenty people. Then after the honeymoon, Mom and Dad will throw us a large reception. The wedding is in July, the reception in August." He took a sip of his cola. "I've already warned Mia that I have a heavy class schedule and an internship at the FBI headquarters downtown. She understands, but I'll help with anything I can."

"Why don't I help as your best woman? If you can't make it to something, then I could always step in. You must keep me in the loop, though."

"Why don't we coordinate our phone. I'll program it so that when Mia sends a text, you can receive it too. But wait ten minutes before you answer. That'll give me time to let her know if I can make it or not."

"Sure." Roc pulled her phone, and they did as he'd suggested. They spent the next few hours catching up on what had been happening in their lives. After Roc left that night, Eagan called Mia and listened to her frustration. He told her about asking Roc to be his best woman and how she had taken the news about their engagement. He fell asleep with a light heart, knowing he'd be seeing the love of his life in less than twelve hours when he picked her up at the airport.

CHAPTER EIGHT
ROCHELLE

Rochelle was livid as she left Eagan's apartment. How dare that fucking cunt bitch agree to marry her man? She didn't know how, and she didn't know when, but she would teach the little whore who was boss. Eagan Davenport was hers. No one took what was hers.

When Eagan had come to her in California over the past summer, she knew her biding her time was working. He'd come crawling back to her. That bullshit of not being romantically attracted to her was just that. Pure and utter bullshit. As she washed her makeup off, it never dawned on her the hour and a half she took to get ready to go to Eagan's apartment with perfect hair, perfect makeup, and a perfect outfit was lost on him. As she climbed into bed, she grabbed her laptop and plotted her revenge. The last words out of her mouth before she fell asleep were. "It will be a cold day in hell when you, little Miss Cuntingham, will marry Eagan Davenport. He's mine and has been for the last twenty-two years."

Starting the next day, Roc made sure she had a full charge on her phone at all times, and it was always within reach. There were texts sent to Eagan, but when they had nothing to do with the wedding, she ignored them, after gagging at their exchanges. Pathetic, that's what they were. Eagan needed a real woman, like Roc, not a little school girl that Mia was.

It wasn't until April that the first text about the wedding came in. It seemed like Mia had stayed in the area over spring break and had been shopping around for cakes, flowers, and venues. Knowing she had no control over the venue, because the discussion had been the wedding would be at the Davenports, she knew she could control the rest. Roc danced with glee when she saw a text come in.

"Hey, E. Can you meet me at two at the cake vendor?"

Roc sent a quick answer. *"What's the address?"*

As soon as she received it, she deleted the text. Shortly after agreeing to be Eagan's best woman for the wedding, she'd befriended a computer geek and told them what they had done about the text. He had shown her how to delete the text before Eagan could see it. So, she did with this set of text messages.

With perfect makeup, tight jeans, and a sexy top, Rochelle walked into the bakery and spotted her target right away. She smiled when Mia gave a start at seeing Rochelle walk through the door. Not wanting to waste any time, she rushed forward, gave Mia an air kiss, and said, "Sorry, Eagan couldn't make it. He asked me to come in his place."

Since Roc knew they had discussed the possibility of Roc filling in for Eagan sometimes, Roc nodded when Mia sighed. "He should have canceled, but this was the only time the baker had available."

"Let's get started then. Since I've known Eagan all his life, I should be able to help with the cake." They looked up when the baker joined them.

"Oh, hello."

"Hi," Roc said, as she held out her hand. "I'm not the groom, but I'm the best woman. The groom couldn't make it and asked me to step in."

"Ah." The baker looked flustered. In five minutes, the two women sat across from each other and tasted the different cake samples. It took everything Roc had not to gag. She hated sweets and avoided them at all costs. She was grateful when the baker left them for a few minutes.

"Here, try this one."

"Can't," Mia said and put her hand over her mouth and nose. "I'm allergic to almonds."

"Oh," Roc frowned, as she put the piece of almond cake with almond frosting down. She picked up another one and made the sounds of enjoying it while trying not to puke. Thank god, there were only eight choices.

"What have you decided?" The baker asked as she returned.

"I really like the lemon, and I know Eagan's favorite pie is lemon. What do you think, Rochelle?"

Roc tried not to cringe at her full name being said by this cunt, but she gritted her teeth and nodded. "You're absolutely right. Lemon is Eagan's favorite."

"Lemon it is." Roc never learned the baker's name, but got her card before she left. "How many people?"

"Only twenty. It'll be a small ceremony. But we'll have a large reception a month later. I'll take your card with me, and depending on my future mother-in-law's recommendation, I may call you."

"Thank you so much." The business cards were passed out, which surprised Roc when Mia whipped out a credit card and paid for it. It also surprised her the address she'd used was Eagan's apartment. Not wanting to be too nosy, she stood there and smiled. It took everything she had not to gag when Mia thanked her and when they parted, Roc hurried into the coffee shop next door, locked herself in the bathroom, and shoved a finger down her throat. She had to get that vile cake out of her system. Eating what she had would throw off her perfect size-four figure. Washing her hands and face, she fixed her makeup, and made her way back out front, picked up a latte, and headed home. It wasn't until one of her friends called that she realized she'd missed an important class. She shrugged. She could always sleep with the TA again to get a good grade. It wouldn't be the first time, and the twit has been hinting he wanted to hook up again.

Three days later, Roc lucked out when she called the bakery and asked for the baker she'd seen earlier in the week. She passed the phone to the teacher's aid she'd been fucking, along with the note she'd written. Roc had blackmailed him into doing this for her. Threatening him if he didn't, she would go to the Dean and tell her that Randy was sexually harassing her. That if she didn't sleep with him, he would give her a failing grade. He was such a sap he fell for it. She had him put it on speaker.

"I'm sorry, she's not here. May I take a message?"

"Please, this is Eagan Davenport calling. My fiancée was in there three days ago and ordered the lemon cake for our wedding in July."

"Oh, yes, I saw the order. Did you want to change it?"

"Yes, please. My fiancée informed me she wanted gluten-free."

"Oh, we can do that."

"How would you do that?"

"We'd use almond flour."

"Is it an additional charge?"

"I don't think so. I can change it if you'd like and send you a copy of the receipt."

"Thank you so much." Randy finished giving the details, and when he hung up, she hugged him and poured them both a glass of victory wine. "I'll get rid of that fucking cunt one way or another, you fucking bitch. Don't mess with me." She downed her wine in only a couple of swallows, then grabbed Randy's hand and pulled him into the bedroom. When he left her apartment three hours later, he wasn't walking steadily.

Two weeks later, she intercepted another text for Eagan to meet Mia at the florist. This time, there was nothing she learned that she could call back and ruin for the bride. But she got the name of the bridal shop Mia would be visiting the following week with her maid of honor. Mia knew that she wouldn't want to invite Eagan to that, so after the visit with the florist, she visited the shop on her own.

Entering the bridal shop, she dismissed the frumpy girl shopping and headed directly to the classy dressed saleswoman.

"May I help you?"

"Yes, my name is Rochelle Mason. I need a wedding dress, but not any dress."

"You know what you want?"

"Yes," Roc waved her hand as she looked down her nose at the saleslady. After all, if she had a job helping others, then she was nothing but a servant. If the bitch didn't want to be treated like one, she should get a proper job. "I'm a size four, I want an above the knee-length white dress, and I mean virginal white. I don't want any pouf shit, or glitter, or bling. I want lace. If it happens to be see-through in places, then all the better. I need to impress the groom at the altar. Oh, and I'm going to need a veil to go with it."

Roc took the glass of champagne offered to her and sat down while the lady got to work. She never saw the frump move to a different location in the store, nor did she care. The servant came out with three dresses and after rejecting two of them, Roc stood to go try on the third. She came out and stood on the small platform. Looking in the mirror, the dress was perfect. It cradled her breasts, and the cut made her look slimmer than her size four. The sides at the waist were missing, so nothing but her skin showed.

"Perfect," Roc said as she twirled around.

"Who's the lucky man?" The lady asked.

"My childhood sweetheart. After being in love for twenty years, he finally asked me to marry him. Of course, I had to say yes. In a little over two months, I'll be Mrs. Eagan Cunningham." Roc sighed as the servant placed a veil on her head and passed her a pair of stunning diamond earrings. "I'll take it."

"So you're saying yes to the dress?"

"Yes," Roc sighed. This was perfect. She couldn't wait to see Eagan's reaction when she stood next to him at the altar. "Eagan's going to fall over when he sees me., shouldn't all grooms look at the love of their lives on their most important day?" She laughed and looked up when the bell on the front door sounded, but shrugged when she saw nothing. The dress had been so perfect that she didn't even have to have any alterations done to it. She couldn't wait for the wedding day. Nothing was going to stop her. Not the fact Eagan was marrying someone else. She had it all planned out. Once the clueless little twit took one bite of the wedding cake, Roc would be there to pick up the pieces of Eagan's broken heart.

CHAPTER NINE
MIA

Mia walked into her dorm room after her last class of the day and collapsed on her bed. All week she'd been taking her mid-term exams, but this last one had been grueling. It had positively drained her. Knowing she should get ready to head over to Eagan's for the weekend, she had just enough energy to send a text telling him she would see him the next day because she was brain dead and didn't trust herself to drive there. Luckily, she knew he would understand, because he had said the same thing to her three days ago. With her phone still in her hand, she fell asleep, sprawled across her bed. She never woke until hours later.

"Hey," Mia said to her roommate as soon as she opened her eyes. "What time is it?"

"Midnight," Heather Grant answered. "Are you okay? You were zonked out when I got in from class."

"I think I'm brain dead," Mia snorted a laugh as she rose from the bed, gathered a set of clothes, and headed toward the bathroom. Twenty minutes later, she emerged, rubbing her stomach. "We have any food here?"

"I ordered a pizza. Thought you'd wake when you smelled it. It's on your desk."

"Thanks." Mia found it, placed two slices on a paper towel, and shoved them in the microwave for a minute. When they finished, she sat crossed legged in the center of her bed and stared at her friend. "Are you okay? You look angry."

"Yeah, I'm good." Heather jumped to her feet, grabbed a bottle of water from their small refrigerator, then settled on the foot of Mia's bed. "Are you awake enough to talk?"

"Sure," she said, around a mouthful of warm pizza. As she ate, she watched the woman who had become her best friend in the last year and a half. Not only were they best friends, but they were roommates, and Mia had asked Heather to be her maid of honor for her upcoming wedding. When Heather continued sitting there, Mia prompted her.

"What's up?"

"How much do you love Eagan?"

"With my whole heart." Mia frowned at the question. She wiped her hands and put the uneaten pizza off to the side. She had a feeling she would not like where this conversation was going.

"Talk to me, Heather. We've told each other almost everything in the last two years. Don't hold back now."

It was several minutes before Heather answered. The first thing she did was jump to her feet to pace. After several rotations, she grabbed Mia's phone from her nightstand and handed it to her. "Your phone rang while you were sleeping. I took it and answered it. I told the caller to call back and leave you a voicemail. Let's start there."

Frowning, Mia took her phone and accessed the voicemail. The more she listened, the wider her eyes became. After she hung up, she looked around frantically. "What time is it?"

"Too late to call back. But there's more."

"What else could there be. Someone called the baker and asked to have my wedding cake made with almond flour. I'm allergic to almonds!"

"I know. I think I know who did it, though."

"Who?"

"Rochelle."

"No way, we buried the hatchet. She even came to the cake testing with me. I had to tell her I was allergic to almonds when she tried to get me to take a sample of the cake with the almond frosting." Mia paused, then frowned. "No, she wouldn't have called to pose as me, would she?"

"I think she would." Heather sat back down on the edge of the bed and grasped Mia's hands in hers. "I knew you were going to busy today with mid-terms. I had several free hours today, so in my excitement, I went to the bridal shop to see what they had."

"Really?" Mia melted at what her friend said.

"Yes, however, when I was there, another customer came in."

"I'm sure they're busy with other brides. I'm not the only one getting married in July."

"I know that, but I recognized the customer. She totally ignored me, and I videoed the interaction with her and the sales lady." Heather pulled her phone, accessed the video, and passed it over to Mia. Before she let it go, she scolded. "Do not, I repeat. Do. Not. Throw. My. Phone." Then she let go and nodded to Mia to push play.

Mia frowned, then watched the video play out. On the screen was Rochelle Mason, giving instructions to the sales lady on the wedding dress she wanted to purchase. At one point in the conversation, when the sales lady asked who the lucky groom was, she froze. Because clear as day, Roc had said Eagan's name. That's when Heather put her hand out and stopped the video.

"Breathe, Mia, breathe. We'll sort this out. But there's more."

Mia watched the tape until the end, then together, they both watched it three more times. Afterward, Mia sat there in stunned silence. It took several minutes for her to wrap her head around what she saw. She looked at Heather and asked, "Can you e-mail me this?"

"Already done."

"Thank you." Mia handed the phone back to Heather and continued to sit there in stunned silence.

Heather whispered, "What are you thinking?"

Giving herself both a mental and physical shake, Mia straightened and stared at her friend. "I will not do anything right now. The first thing I want to do is to talk to Eagan. He knows my feelings about her. But I think I can come up with something to prove to Eagan that she's lying."

"What's that?"

"When I see him later today, I'm going to see if he can get her to come over. Wedding business." Mia grinned at Heather's raised brow. Her expression caused Heather to shudder.

"What would be the purpose of that?"

"I'm going to ask her what she's going to wear to the wedding."

"Ah, see if she's lying or not."

"Correct. Then I can talk about the cake, I don't know what I'll say yet, but I'll think of something."

"Does Eagan know you're allergic to almonds?"

"Yes."

"Man, I'd love to be a fly on the wall for the conversation with that bitch."

"Come with."

"Excuse me?"

"If I'm going to tell Eagan to have her there to talk about the wedding, shouldn't my maid of honor be there also?"

"Oh, I like that. The only plan I have is to do my laundry, but I can do that anytime this weekend. I'm in." They giggled and took notes about everything Roc had done or said since Mia met Eagan. They ended up staying up all night and doing their laundry together, along with cleaning their room. So, when it was time for Mia to leave to head over to Eagan's apartment for the rest of the weekend, their chores were completed. They were a little tired, but with a bracing cup of extra strong coffee, they were ready to go.

MIA WAITED BESIDE HER car for Heather to park, and together they headed toward the elevator that would lead them to Eagan's apartment.

"I'm not staying long," Heather said on their way up. "I want to hear what she's going to wear."

"Yeah, me too. I know we talked about it, but if I distract Eagan in a different room, could you set up a camera?"

"Sure," Heather said as she patted her purse. Her major was computer science, so she could write, decipher, and break code, but she also dabbled in a video class on the side. She'd contacted Gregory, and he'd hooked her up with some state-of-the-art equipment.

Instead of knocking on the door, Mia used her key and smiled when she entered and saw Eagan pouring himself a cup of coffee. They both immediately went to one another and kissed. Neither one heard Heather's sigh in the background.

"I missed you," Eagan said as he put his hands on her hips and held her to him. "I don't know about you, but it's been a hell of a week for me."

"Me too," Mia sighed as she put her forehead on her chest, and just breathed him in. "Sorry about last night, but when I got back to my room after my last mid-term, I was so brain dead, I didn't want to chance driving over."

"Not a problem. I ended up working late at the FBI office. I never got in until almost midnight." Eagan smiled, then looked up at their guest. "Hey, Heather, nice to see you? Coffee?" He walked back to the kitchen and took down two cups.

"Sure."

"Have you heard from Davis lately?"

"No, have you?"

"Not since the last time you and I talked. I'm sure he'll contact you when he can."

"Yeah, that's what I think too. I hate that he's over there. I know he's doing great things, but I miss him."

"I'm sure you do." He passed the coffee out, then with his hand around Mia's, he smiled. "It's good you brought Heather. I agree we should nail some details about the wedding down. When you sent the text, you were on your way. I called Roc to get her over here."

"Is she coming?" Heather asked.

"Yes, but knowing her, she'll take two hours to drive five minutes." He shook his head, then looked at Mia. "I've received some invoices. I believe they're for the wedding. Come into my spare room, to see if they are."

Mia took that opportunity to nod to Heather. With them looking at the invoices, Heather could set up the cameras to aim them at the kitchen and the living room's seating area. Luckily, they were only small units, shaped and sized like a pencil. Gregory had set their feed up to run on Heather's computer back in the dorm. He had taken the laptop and made sure to monitor it. Heather only had to text him when Roc arrived. The only thing they needed to remember was to grab them when they left.

"These came in the mail," Eagan said as he sat at his desk, and pulled her into his lap. Together they opened them, and when he read them, he passed them over. "I'm not reading them word for word. I'm looking at the bottom line."

"Why? I told you Dad gave me a credit card. I'm staying well within my limit."

"I know that, and I'm not questioning that. I'm making sure they're paid in full. You know I'll pay for anything extra."

"Oh," Mia said. "Do you mind if I take these?"

"Not at all. You have a folder set up, don't you?"

"I do." She stuffed the invoices back into their envelopes to put in her purse. Back out in the living room, Mia saw Heather's grin, and they settled in the living room to wait for Roc. An hour later, she knocked on the front door. Because Mia was closer, she opened the door. It took everything she had not to slap the bitch across the face. Instead, she smirked at the other woman when she gave a startled gasp seeing Mia at the door.

"What are you doing here?" Roc demanded.

"Visiting *my* fiancé," she stressed, then stepped back, not bothering to say hello.

"Where's Eagan?"

"Here," he called as he joined them, and wrapped his arm around Mia's waist. When Roc tried to hug him, he held out his hand instead. His actions made Mia feel ten feet tall. It took everything Mia had not to laugh at the expression of annoyance on Roc's face at Eagan's treatment of her. Instead, she acted as the woman of the house, and said, "Rochelle, thank you for coming. Since we're all here, Eagan and I thought it would be good to nail down any last-minute details about the wedding."

"What's to nail down?" Roc frowned, and when she tried to sit next to Eagan, he switched seats with Heather and sat in a chair instead of on the couch. Pulling Mia into his lap.

"I've ordered the cake and the flowers," Mia began. "Both Eagan and I decided not to have a meal. We're only having hors d'oeuvres. Meg said she and David would take care of those."

"You're calling Eagan's parents by their given names?" Roc asked in shock.

"Why wouldn't she?" Eagan demanded. "She's about to be their daughter."

"Oh." Eagan's statement seemed to take some wind out of her sails. "If you have the cake, flowers, and food at the reception, what else does it leave?"

"Our attire. I, of course, will be in a white gown. Heather, as my maid of honor, will wear a pale purple dress. Eagan, of course, will be in a black tux, with a pale green cummerbund, and his boutonniere will match a sprig of my flowers. Since you are the best woman, Eagan and I would like you to wear a gray tux, with the purple cummerbund and matching boutonniere."

Mia winged it as she spoke. She had never discussed what Rochelle would wear at the wedding. She had thought to leave it up to Eagan to tell her. But after watching that video from earlier, she took the bull by the horns. With no clue what Eagan's thoughts were, but she would love Eagan to the day she died for his next words.

"I agree. I think that would be perfect. Being the bride and groom, Mia and I will be in black and white. I think the gray and purple will offset the two of us and complement the two of you. I don't care if you wear a skirt or pants, but I agree with the gray."

Heather took up the conversation then, "I think it would be perfect. We can even go together the day before the wedding to get mani/pedis."

"Who the fuck are you?" Rochelle glared at Heather.

"I'm the maid of honor."

Rochelle glared at her. She looked over at Eagan, and said, "Eagan, can we step outside and discuss this?"

"Why? Mia's the bride. If you have something to say about her ideas, then she needs to hear them. I won't leave Mia out of any conversations about the wedding."

Mia had been watching Roc closely, and smirked when she realized how good she was, but because of that scrutiny, Mia saw the tightening around her eyes and lips. She glanced at Heather, and they nodded as each of them saw it.

"I'll take into consideration what you said and get back to you."

"Get back to us about what?" Mia asked.

"The color of my tux."

"Do you really have a say?" Heather asked. "Isn't it up to the bride to pick out the colors *she* wants at *her* wedding?"

"Eagan," Rochelle whined.

"What? This is Mia's and my day. If she wants you to wear gray, then you'll wear gray." Eagan frowned at his friend. His next statement played right into Mia's hands. "If you don't want to do as the bride wishes, I can always have my dad stand up for me. I know he has a perfect gray suit he can wear."

"I'll do it," she admitted after several minutes of silence. Then she jumped to her feet. "I gotta go." She left before anyone could say anything. The three of them sat there in stunned silence for several minutes.

"I think that went well," Eagan said as he picked Mia up, and put her on her feet before standing. He didn't see the rolled eye expression Heather and Mia made to one another. "I'll be right back." Eagan left the room, and Heather hurried to gather the two pencil cameras she'd set up earlier. She had just stuck them in her purse when Eagan returned.

"Sorry to be a party pooper, but I'm going to head out, too. I've got a ton of studying to do and a lot of laundry."

"How many exams do you have left?"

"Two on Monday, and one on Tuesday. Then I'm done."

"Good luck." Eagan walked her to the door. After they hugged, he shut and locked the door. With a grin on his face, he asked. "So, what shall we do with the rest of our weekend?"

"Do you have to work for your internship?"

"Nope, because I worked late last night, I'm done now until Wednesday."

"Do you have to study?"

"If I don't know it by now, then I might as well hang it up." Eagan grinned. "I'm the type of person who reads the notes before entering class. I've seemed to ace all my tests that way."

"Good for you." She walked around, then turned, and with her hands twisted in front of her, she bit her lower lip and stared at him.

"What?"

"I know I said I want to wait, but how would you feel if we have our wedding night now?"

Mia watched Eagan stare at her in stunned silence before a massive grin came over his face. "And to think, I stopped on my way home and bought condoms."

"Really?"

"Yep," he said as he walked forward, took her face in his hands, and kissed her deeply.

CHAPTER TEN
EAGAN

Eagan stared at Mia in shock. She stood before him, biting her lower lip, which always caused him to harden. He couldn't wait to get those lips wrapped around his cock again. They'd been doing a lot of oral sex in the last few months, and the sight of her biting her lip turned him on, but he didn't want to push her into anything she wasn't ready for. Seeing her stare at him with those doe-like eyes, biting her lower lip, and twisting her fingers together, he couldn't believe his luck.

Stepping forward, he gathered her face in his hands, looked deep into her eyes, and whispered, "Are you sure?"

She swallowed several times, licked her lips, then nodded. "Yes, I'm sure."

Not wanting to look a gift horse in the mouth, Eagan swooped in and kissed her. This wasn't one of their regular kisses. If she wanted to hit a home run, then he would pour all his passion for her into his kiss. She must have liked it, because she wrapped her hands around his neck and stepped further into their embrace. Several minutes later, they both broke apart, panting.

"If you're sure, then let's move this to the bedroom," Mia told him.

"I'm sure. I'm going to make certain we lock the door."

"Okay." He walked to the door, towing Mia behind them. Now that she had finally agreed to have sex with him, he would not let go of her. After he double-checked the deadbolt, along with the handle lock, for good measure, he put the chain on. When Mia giggled from beside him, he looked at her and grinned.

"Can never be too safe," he smirked when Mia laughed at him. Without a word, he squeezed her hand tighter and pulled her behind him as he headed toward the bedroom. Once inside, he turned and closed that door. "I know it's only eleven in the morning, but I can't wait for this."

"I know. But I need to tell you, when I came home from school yesterday I was brain dead and fell asleep. I woke at midnight, but couldn't get back to sleep. Heather and I cleaned our room and did our weekend chores. I guess what I'm trying to say is that I've been up since midnight."

"Do you want to take a nap before we do this?"

"Do you want to wait?"

"Hell, no." Eagan stared at her in mock outrage, swooped down, and kissed her. As he did, he backed them up, so when her knees hit the bed, he followed her down. He broke off the kiss long enough to say. "I've wanted this since the day I first met you. There is so much I want to do with you. Since it's your first time, I'll only do the basics."

"Isn't that all there is?"

"Not by a long shot," Eagan laughed. He kissed her and ran his hand under her shirt, and didn't stop until he lifted her bra to cradle her breasts. Lifting his head, he looked at her. "We've played before, but not intensely."

"If not intensely, what do you call the oral sex we've been having?"

"Fine, I guess it was intense." He grinned at her. "This time, when I go down on you, you'll get nice and wet so I can slip inside."

"Are you going to fit? Because we both know you barely fit in my mouth."

"Oh, yeah, I'll fit." He grinned, and in only a couple of moves, he had both her shirt and bra off along with his own shirt. Eagan loved the feel of Mia's skin. Every chance he had, he liked to caress it. The silky smoothness reminded him of sunshine and roses. He would forever associate those smells with her smooth skin. Leaving her lips, he kissed his way over to her ear and nuzzled the spot he knew drove her wild. With one hand wrapped around her breast, he moved his other down to undo her jeans. In seconds, his hand slipped inside her panties. Eagan sighed against her skin when he felt how wet she was.

"As much as I want to take my time with you, I don't know if I can wait."

"No one's asking you to." Mia sighed against his neck. She loved what he was doing to her. Impatient to get things rolling, she reached out, undid his jeans, and grasped his hard length in her hand. Giving it a hard squeeze, she knew he liked.

"Slow down, or I won't last," he murmured against her neck.

"Then, you better hurry." Mia groaned as she threw her head back and bucked her hips into his hand. He worked her into a frenzy by pinching her clit. In seconds, her first orgasm overtook her. Mia lost all track of time after that. It wasn't until she returned to her senses, she realized they were both naked, and Eagan hovered above her.

"Condom?"

"Already on, you back with me?"

"Hmm." She smiled up at him, wrapped her arms around his neck, and her legs around his waist. "I know it's going to hurt, but I'm okay with that."

"I'll be gentle," Eagan whispered, as he worked the head of his cock into her entrance. Knowing she was a virgin, he went as slow as he could. When he reached the barrier, he paused, pulled out, and eased back in. Mia's next move surprised him. When he backed off, she tightened her grip with her legs, and as he eased back in, she slammed her hips up, allowing him to break through. Both of them cried out as he sank in as far as he could go.

"Christ," Eagan said into her hair. "Why did you do that?" He had a hard time talking. It took everything he had not to come. "God, you're so tight."

"You were taking too long," Mia groaned, and used her inner muscles to squeeze him.

"Don't, or I'm going to come right now."

Mia froze, then smiled up at him. The look on his face said he was in a combination of bliss and pain. Before she could say anything, he opened one eye and grinned at her. "Remind me to spank your ass for that move later."

Laughing, Mia said, "Yeah, I'll put a pin in it." Laughing, Eagan moved and closed his eyes in pure sexual bliss.

"You feel amazing." They spoke no more words for several minutes. At least, not until Eagan screamed, "Again, Mia! Come again!" He reached between them and pinched her clit.

As soon as she felt the bite of pain, she threw her head back and screamed her orgasm. Eagan was right there with her. Both breathed heavily as they tried to regain their composure. Rolling over, Eagan brought Mia with him and wrapped her in his arms.

"That was amazing, and you were too. Give me about an hour, and we can go again." He smirked at her and chuckled softly when he realized she was asleep. Knowing she'd been up for twelve hours, Eagan slipped from the bed, and after a quick shower, went out to the living room, giving Mia the rest she needed. Before leaving the bedroom, he looked down at her, and his heart swelled with love for her.

TWO HOURS LATER, EAGAN looked up from the book he was reading, and smiled as Mia entered the room wearing only his t-shirt. "Nice nap?"

"Yes, how long did I sleep?"

"Two hours," he said as he rose, gathered her in his arms, and held her tight. "Thank you for earlier. I tried to tell you, but you'd fallen asleep."

"God, I'm so sorry."

"Don't worry about it. It means it was good for you." He grinned and brought her to the kitchen. "I have some soup if you're hungry?"

Before Mia could answer, her stomach growled, causing them both to laugh. As Eagan fixed her lunch, he said, "Your phone has been ringing off the hook. I didn't answer, but I thought I'd let you know."

Mia frowned, went to her purse, and dug out her phone. She saw several missed calls from Heather. They coordinated with the number of voicemails. As she listened, she walked down the hall for privacy. After the first one, she went into the bedroom, dressed, and returned.

"Sorry, but I'm not hungry."

"What's wrong?" Eagan frowned, seeing her expression, and frowned when he noticed she had dressed. He had planned to spend the rest of the afternoon in bed with her.

"I need to talk to you about something, and I'm saying you will not like it." To get through this conversation, Mia had to firm her resolve to confront Eagan. Her tone might have come across as a little bitchy.

Eagan frowned. "Not with that attitude, I won't." He crossed his arms and glared at her. When she refused to say anything, he lifted his chin toward her. "Go ahead, I'm listening."

Mia took a deep breath and said as clearly as her shaking body could. "I don't want Rochelle at the wedding."

"Too bad, she's my best friend, and I want her there."

"And if I don't want her there?"

"You'll live with it. I said nothing earlier when you sprung the fact that you wanted Roc to wear a gray tux, but I won't back down on this."

"Then I'm calling the wedding off," Mia said, and removed her engagement ring. At his stunned look, she held her head high. She backed toward the door, picking up her purse on the way. "Last chance. If she's in, I'm out."

"Bullshit, I'm calling your bluff."

"Fine." Mia turned to the door and unlocked the three locks. She opened it, then turned back to him. "Talk to your so-called best friend. I dare you. I refuse to allow that bitch at my wedding. Not when I have proof that she's trying to kill me."

"I'm calling bullshit again," Eagan screamed at her. "Roc would never hurt anyone that I love. You can't call off the wedding because I want my best friend in it! I want to know what the fuck is going on!"

"Fine! You want details? I'll give you the details." Mia screamed as she pulled the envelopes from earlier, stormed over to him, and threw them at him. He never flinched when they hit his chest and fell to the ground. "Those are for starters. Why the fuck would you call and have the baker put almond flour in our wedding cake?"

"What? What are you talking about? I never did that?"

"But your best friend did!" Mia was screaming now. "When she showed up at the cake tasting, because you couldn't make it, she tried to get me to eat a piece with almond frosting."

"What cake tasting? I don't know what you're talking about."

"I sent you a text about it! She showed up and said, you couldn't make it."

"I never received a text about it." Eagan frowned and grabbed his phone. Mia accessed hers and showed him.

"Crap, I think I know what happened."

"What's that?" Mia wasn't about to back down. It was Roc or her.

"When I asked Roc to be my best woman, we set it up so that any text coming from you went to her phone. I told her to fill in for me if I couldn't make it."

"You did what?" Mia screamed. She was livid! "Are you telling me every text I sent you for the last four months she's received! Even the sex ones?"

Eagan had the good grace to blush. "Apparently so." His only response was a shrug.

"And that doesn't bother you?"

"Not really, it's just Roc."

"Oh my god, you are so delusional with that bitch."

"Please don't call her that. She's my best friend."

Mia snorted a laugh and shook her head. "Fine, let me tell you what your best friend has done. Not only have you allowed her to spy on us by including her in our private text messages, but she's also gone to the point of contacting the baker to request the wedding cake be made with almond flour. And!" Mia had to pause to control her voice. Her body was shaking so hard, it made her voice shake. "Your so-called best friend went to the bridal shop and purchased a wedding dress to wear to the wedding. That's why I told her I wanted her in a gray tux!"

Eagan scoffed at her, "Roc would never do that."

"What about taking our personal text messages and putting them all over the campus website? Or the fact that she contacted your mother and said because she was your best woman, she requested some shit made with almonds for the reception? Or that she contacted the florist and had the baby's breath in my bouquet switched out to almond blossoms? Or what about the fact that she's telling everyone she's pregnant, and you're the father? Have you fucked her since we've been together?"

"What the fuck are you talking about, lady! I know you don't like Roc, but that's no reason to make up lies about my best friend. I've known her for twenty-two years, and you for only seventeen months."

"So, she's staying in the wedding?"

"Yes, I won't listen to your lies." Eagan crossed his arms over his chest, stood tall, and glared at his fiancée.

"Fine, have a nice life with the fucking bitch." Mia said calmly. So calmly that Eagan felt a chill run down his spine. "I'll give you forty-eight hours to think this over. If you still agree to have her in the wedding, then I'm still calling it off." Without another word, Mia stormed out of the open door and shut it so quietly behind her, the soft click sounded like a cannon going off.

Eagan became so pissed, he picked up the pot of soup he'd heated and threw it against the wall. Then he whipped open the refrigerator and grabbed a beer, downing it in three swallows. He grabbed another one. He lost count after the sixth one.

How dare Mia spread those lies about Roc? Never in a million years would his best friend ever do what Mia was accusing her of.

EPILOGUE

Forty-eight hours later, Mia let herself into Eagan's apartment at eleven o'clock on Monday morning. She was only there to get the rest of her stuff. The only contact with him she'd had since storming out on Saturday had been a clipped text to tell him to open his e-mail. She never knew if he received it or not. That bitch Roc probably deleted it before he could see it. Mia had told Heather what Eagan told her about the text messages. To Mia's horror, Heather confirmed that it could be done. After returning to her own dorm room, she'd packed up all her things. Afterward, Mia drove around town and canceled everything she had done for the wedding.

Luckily, since she was still within the time limits, each place could refund her credit card. That was going to make her father happy. What would not make him happy would be the outcome of her meeting with Eagan today. If Eagan continued to insist on Roc being innocent, she was so done with him, and Mia would probably head for home. With only a few weeks left, she'd finish her classes online and have the university mail her degree to her. She refused to attend the same college with those two if he allowed Roc at the wedding. It was her or me situation. Because of everything Roc had done, Mia was ninety-nine-point-nine-nine-percent sure Eagan would pick the bitch over her. The woman he claimed he loved with all his heart.

Entering the apartment, Mia paused, then leaned back out to make sure she had the right one. The ordinarily immaculate apartment was in shambles. There were beer bottles and takeout containers all over the living room and kitchen island. At first glance, it looked like Eagan had a party and never cleaned up from it. The further into the apartment, the messier it became. After walking around the place to make sure she had all her own things she'd left there over the weeks of staying on the weekends, she headed to his bedroom. Since he should be in class, she had no reason to worry.

Opening the bedroom door, Mia stopped dead in her tracks. Seeing red, she walking into the adjoining bathroom, grabbed the glass Eagan kept on the sink and filled it with ice water. She then went back out and threw it on the two people sleeping naked in the bed.

"What the fuck?" Eagan sputtered as he jerked up and stared at her. "What the fuck did you do that for?"

"What the fuck are you in bed with her for?" Mia shot back, and pointed to Rochelle as she used the corner of the sheet, not covering her, and wiped the water from her face. Mia noticed Roc wore the engagement ring that Mia had left here two days ago.

"You couldn't even wait the forty-eight hours, could you?"

"What the fuck are you talking about?" Eagan acted like he had no clue what was going on.

"I see you gave the bitch my ring. Don't worry, since you've sided with her, the wedding's off. Never contact me again," Mia said through gritted teeth. She stormed out, but returned seconds later. "Before I go, I need to do something. I've wanted to do for the last seventeen months." Without a word, she walked over to the side of the bed that used to be Mia's, balled up her fist, and let it fly. When Rochelle's head snapped back, and the back of her head hit the headboard, Mia took satisfaction in the fact her eye started turning blue immediately. She turned on her heel and left. Mia knew she would never love another man as she did Eagan. It would be a long time before she would ever get over him.

EAGAN NEVER MOVED UNTIL he heard the slam of the front door. He then turned to stare in horror at his best friend.

"What the fuck are you doing in my bed?" He jumped to his feet and sighed in relief when he realized he still had his jeans on. But Roc threw the covers back and stood, totally naked. The last thing he remembered was Mia storming out, him throwing the pan of soup against the wall, and grabbing a beer. Disgusted, he turned and didn't look at Roc as she dressed. When she finished, he turned back around.

"Answer me, what the fuck are you doing naked in my bed?"

"Don't you remember calling me and asking me to come over? We had such wonderful sex."

"Bullshit," Eagan spat. "I know that's a lie, because I can't get hard around you." He finally rubbed the water from his face and frowned at his massive headache. Eagan stormed into the bathroom and grabbed some pain pills, downing them, then went to the kitchen to make coffee. When Roc joined him, he reached out and jerked her left hand toward him. After wrenching the ring from her finger, he glared at her.

"Why are you here?" When he saw her look around, he crossed his arms and glared. "Don't lie to me. Did you have someone call and put almond flour in my wedding cake? Did you call Mom to have almonds added to the food?" When she still refused to answer, he sighed. "You know, I only have to make one phone call." He picked up his phone, and she broke.

"Yes, all right, I did it."

"Why?"

"Because that fucking cunt bitch came between us!" She screamed at him.

"There is no us. There never has been and never will be! When are you going to get that through your thick skull! You fucking ruined the best thing that ever happened to me. I want you out of my life." Eagan shook as he lifted his arm and pointed to his apartment door. "I mean it, I never want to see you ever again, Rochelle. If you even contact my parents, I'll slap a restraining order on you so fast, you won't know what hit you!"

"But, I love you, Eagan!" Rochelle whined. "I've loved you since we were two years old. You're lucky I allowed you to date Sue Ellen in high school. I only did it to let you sow your wild oats. I knew once we were together here at college, you would fall in love with me."

"You're sick. I never believed Sue Ellen or Mia, but now I understand where they're coming from. I want you gone. Never contact me again. Not in person, on the phone, or through social media. You turned a friendship into something ugly. You turn my stomach." He turned his back on her, waiting for her to leave.

"You'll regret this, Eagan. You love me. I know it. Don't do this to us."

"There is no us. Get the fuck out of my life. I have so much to repair because of you."

"No one will come between us again." Roc tried to touch him, but he jerked away and pulled out his phone.

"You have ten seconds to leave, or I call 9-1-1 and tell them you broke in uninvited. How would that look on your transcript going to Harvard? Get the fuck out of my life, Rochelle," he repeated, and sighed when she finally took the hint. At the door, she turned and what she said turned his skin to ice.

"I'll have you one day, Eagan Davenport. No one will ever love you like I do. You are my one and only. Just remember that your precious Mia's lucky she got out alive. The next one won't." Then she walked out, slamming the door behind her.

Eagan spent the rest of the afternoon cleaning his apartment. Because he had a final the next day, he studied for that. Afterward, he called his supervisor at his internship and had the rest of the week off. He remained holed up in his apartment until it was time to return to classes. The only time he ventured out was to knock on Mia's door. Only to find her irate roommate giving him a piece of unsolicited advice. Heather told him to check his e-mail. Afterward, he became incensed with what he'd learned about his now ex-best friend.

Weeks later, after the last final exam of his college career, he packed up his apartment and drove home. Graduation was in two weeks, but he wouldn't be attending. He had even talked to the Dean about it. Next was to discuss his career choice with his parents.

"EAGAN, WHAT ARE YOU doing here?" his mother asked, when he walked in the back door to his childhood home late Wednesday night.

"I'm done with college." He set his bag down, hugged his mother, and shook his father's hand.

"So, what now?"

"That's what I'm here to talk to you about. First, the wedding is still off. I'll get into that later." He rubbed his face, then sighed. "No, I better tell you now. When Mia and I fought about Rochelle, I took Rochelle's side."

Eagan didn't see his parents exchange looks, because he had never called Roc by her given name unless he was mad at her.

"What happened?"

"Turned out, Mia was right all along. I feel so stupid now. Throughout high school, everyone always told me Rochelle was in love with me. Turned out they were right. I classified her as a best friend. That was all. Since Mia broke up with me, I've learned that Rochelle broke into our mailbox here, and found my acceptance letter to UB, then she applied."

"Ah, so that's why she didn't go to Berkley?" his father asked, as he handed his son a bottle of beer.

"Correct. I've also learned that since agreeing to be my best woman for the wedding, she undermined all of Mia's decisions."

"How?" Both parents asked together.

"Mia is allergic to almonds. Rochelle had someone call the baker and request almond flour for the cake. Turned out it was a man calling and said he was me. I learned it was a TA, she's been sleeping with him to get passing grades. She threatened to go to the Dean if he didn't do it."

"Damn." Meg looked at her son in shock. "Oh, shit, she called here and requested several dishes that called for almonds. She said they were Mia's favorite."

"She lied. Mia is deadly allergic to almonds. I've had to rush her to the hospital once. It's not pretty."

"Wow." David shook his head. "What else?"

"Rochelle went to the bridal shop and bought a wedding dress, to wear to the wedding when she stood as the best woman. Trust me, it's true. When I'm not so pissed, I'll show you the video. The nail on her coffin was when Mia came to talk to me, and she found Rochelle in bed with me wearing Mia's ring."

"You didn't?"

"No, I was so fucking drunk that I was out of it for two days. Rochelle says I called her, and when she showed up, she put me to bed. Thank god nothing happened."

"So, what are you going to do now?" David asked.

"I've talked to the Dean, and I won't be at graduation."

"Why not?" Meg frowned at her son. "You've worked so hard for that degree.

"I know, but in seventy-two hours, I'm climbing on a bus and heading to Parris Island, South Carolina."

"What's there?" David frowned at his son. He knew, but he didn't want to voice his concerns. He only reached over and grabbed his wife's hand.

"Marine Corps boot camp. I've joined the Marines. I need to get away from Rochelle. I figured this would be the best way, besides serving my country. I'm going to make a vow right now.

CLAIMING MIA

I claimed Mia once, and I don't care how long it takes. I'll claim her again. She is the love of my life. If joining the Marines will help clear my head, then so be it. But mark my words, Mia Angelique Cunningham will be mine once again.

THE END

If you enjoyed Claiming Mia, the next book, Re-Claiming Mia is available for pre-order. Pick up your copy today.

Thank you for taking the time to read this. If you enjoyed this book, please give it some love and leave a review at your preferred site.

You can contact me at:

E-mail: deannalrowley@yahoo.com

Facebook: https://www.facebook.com/Author-Deanna-L-Rowley-106623544172360

Website: https://deannalrowley.com/

Newsletter: https://cheerful-artisan-8318.ck.page/

AGAIN, THANK YOU FOR taking the time to read this.

Also by:

LOVE FOUND SERIES

LOVE DOESN'T EXIST: https://books2read.com/u/3GMqA8
Love Is Fleeting: https://books2read.com/u/3JK11P
Love Conquers All: https://books2read.com/u/b5x2Al

SPIES, LIES & RIDES

Aimee's Dilemma: https://books2read.com/u/boEXvp

Hank's Mission: https://books2read.com/u/bQKQew

Colt's Quest: https://books2read.com/u/boEKdp

The rest of the series coming in 2021

George's Goal
Hogan's Handful
Witt's Warrior's
John's Journey
Gary's Turn

STORMVILLE – SUSPENSEFUL SEDUCTION WORLD

Samantha A. Cole's Trident Security Books
Bourbon Blaze https://books2read.com/u/baakP6
Neil's Wish https://books2read.com/u/mZakwl[1]
Ginny's Slow Sizzle https://books2read/u/mowozo
Max and Claire's story continues in the CAPE Investigations Series
Coming in 2021
Claiming Mia
Re-Claiming Mia
Protecting Claire
Challenging Claire
Taming Sue Ellen

---

1. https://books2read.com/u/mZakwl

Forgiving Heather
Defending Melody
Saving Kate
Coming March 9th, 2021
In
Susan Stoker's Universe
Saving Veronica
Coming April 13, 2021
in
Elle James' Brotherhood Protection World
Morgan

Coming in 2022
Not Her Series:
Not Her Dom
Not Her Choice
Not Her Rebound
Not Her Problem #1
Not Her Fault
Not Her Problem #2
Not Her Doing
LINKS TO FOLLOW WHEN uploaded for pre-order

ABOUT THE AUTHOR

Deanna has loved to read all her life. She was in the third grade when she fell in love with books while working in the school library. She turned that love of reading into writing. Now Deanna can be found either in her writing cave, sharing her keyboard with her furbaby, reading, or making quilts.

Don't miss out!

Visit the website below and you can sign up to receive emails whenever Deanna L. Rowley publishes a new book. There's no charge and no obligation.

https://books2read.com/r/B-A-WBNL-KMYMB

BOOKS 2 READ

Connecting independent readers to independent writers.

www.ingramcontent.com/pod-product-compliance
Lightning Source LLC
Chambersburg PA
CBHW071208130726
47998CB00002B/667